TURKEY HASH

Novels by Craig Nova

TURKEY HASH
THE GEEK
INCANDESCENCE
THE GOOD SON
THE CONGRESSMAN'S DAUGHTER
TORNADO ALLEY

TURKEY HASH

CRAIG NOVA

A Delta Book
Published by
Dell Publishing
a division of
Bantam Doubleday Dell Publishing Group, Inc.
666 Fifth Avenue
New York, New York 10103

I would like to express my gratitude for the assistance provided by the National Foundation for the Arts.—C.N.

ISBN: 0-385-29719-X

Reprinted by arrangement with the author

Printed in the United States of America

Published simultaneously in Canada

May 1989
10 9 8 7 6 5 4 3 2 1

BG

Turkey Hash: This is the delight of all connoisseurs of the holiday beast, but few understand how really to prepare it. Like a lobster, it must be plunged alive into boiling water, until it becomes bright red or purple or something, and then before the color fades, placed quickly in a washing machine and allowed to stew in its own gore as it is whirled around. Only then is it ready for hash. To hash, take a large sharp tool like a nail-file or, if none is handy, a bayonet will serve the purpose—and then get at it! Hash it well! Bind the remains with dental floss and serve.

F. SCOTT FITZGERALD
The Crack-Up

Los Angeles

H er yellow teeth are hard. I know: they gnaw my fingers as I try to catch the slippery tongue. She looks surprised, then collapses like a palsied guard, strikes her head against the glass tabletop. A swollen and peevish face, so much like a formaldehyde child's. I think of bits of floating flesh, a scene from some snowy paperweight.

Don't eat yourself, I think, don't swallow it.

Her rigid flesh bounces against the floor, over slivers as sharp and clear as bits of shattered icicle. I mop greenish froth and blood with an awkward ball of toilet paper, but bits of glass cling to it, cut her face.

In the morning, shock-warm, she stands in the hall. "What are you doing in my house?" says Burned. Epileptic hands have drawn a mouth around her own, an ugly parody of sensuality. A stocking bunches around one knee like the top of a seven-league boot.

"What are you doing in my house?"

"It's Niles. Niles," I say, "your son."

"Oh?" she says, fingering the cut above her brow, glancing into my room where she sees the stained ball of toilet paper on my bureau. "Oh, Niles, what time do I have to get up this morning?"

One-eyed Horsetrader stands in his yard as Sis, Rodeorider, and I pull up in a purple '56 Chevrolet. Rodeorider, Sis's boyfriend, always sits down slowly because some of the bones in his ass are broken. Horsetrader looks at the purple Chevrolet and then at us. Beyond the back lot and over the shoulder of the barn I see the ladderlike structures and heavy pipes of the steam plant. Air smells like it had leaked out of a radiator.

"I'll talk," says Rodeorider.

Sis smiles and it makes Rodeorider mad.

"He can hardly count," whispers Sis to me. When she smiles I can see a tooth of hers that's turning gray. Rodeorider said "Eyetalian" once, and Sis laughed at him. He carries Police Special, a .38, in the glove box, waiting for someone to give him shit on the freeway.

Horsetrader's just standing in his yard thinking about money the way most men sit in the shade.

"You ain't so smart," I say to her. She looks into my eyes and scratches my arm from elbow to hand, but I don't blink.

"Don't you touch her, Niles," says Rodeorider.

Horsetrader's got a wad of moist cotton in his blind socket, and every now and then he pushes it farther into the hole.

"You got a pig?" asks Rodeorider.

Horsetrader's house slouches in the yard. Through the screen door I can see his pale Oklahoma wife and kids. Steam plant sighs, quietly fills the air with billows of white silk. Horsetrader's wad pushes the lids and lashes into the socket. I try to pet his dog, but it snaps.

"You got a pig?" asks Rodeorider. He wears a western shirt, sharply scalloped over the shoulders, front, and cuffs, spotted with buttons of mother-of-pearl. Cowboy boots, jeans, and a buckle he won at a rodeo in Sagus. You should see Sagus.

"I got a pig," says Horsetrader.

Sis looks at the horse in the corral. Crooked lip tries to cover that graying tooth.

"Get out of the car," she says, pushing me against the door. "What are you waiting for?"

Horsetrader looks mean, but it's part of his style, I guess. He's got a hand-tooled wallet in his back pocket, and it's fastened to his belt by a silver chain. He sees me looking at it and says, "Pickpockets. They got 'em at the auction." One eye cuts his smile in half.

"Let's have a look at him," says Rodeorider.

I'm still trying to make friends with Horsetrader's dog, but he's not having any.

"That's a eating dog," says Horsetrader.

Sis's hands are cracked and a little scabby because she washes them a lot. They itch, too, and she scratches at them. This pig was her idea. Horsetrader's dog looks at my outstretched fingers and curls his lip.

"What's wrong with those hands, girlie?" asks Horsetrader.

"Nothing," says Rodeorider.

Come on, doggie, got a Mars bar in my pocket.

"For Christ's sake," says Rodeorider, "leave him alone."

"Pig's over here," says Horsetrader.

Rodeorider's purple Chevrolet's got steer horns and a chrome horse on the hood, sparkly mud flaps behind the rear wheels, and real cowhide seats. When Rodeorider and Sis go driving, she reaches in his pants, moves her hands up and down. That's all they ever do. But Burned counts Sis's underwear and says, There's one missing. Did you leave it on the floor of that Chevrolet?

"No one'd try to pick his pocket," Sis whispers to me. "He hasn't got any money. He's lying."

The pen, behind the barn, is made of old, moist wood with soft splinters that crumble against my hand. The pig's black and white, about five feet long, as tall as a big dog. On his black marking there's whitish soot from the steam plant. He doesn't look mean, just lazy.

"Looks like he's dead," says Rodeorider.

"Naw," says Horsetrader.

Pig, in the corner of his pen, has his nose in a pile of yellowish shit. He flaps his ears every now and then and looks around, but when he sees Horsetrader he jerks his eyes away.

"He looks sick," says Sis.

"Naw," says Horsetrader.

He waits, nostrils quivering as he smells the damp air, one eye snapping every now and then toward Sis's hands. Rodeorider doesn't have anything to say so he squints for a while. I wonder about Sis's hands, whether they'll make Pig cost more or less. Valves in the steam plant click. Rodeorider takes a piece of aspirin gum out of his pocket and puts it into his mouth. Rodeorider chews aspirin gum all day.

"I'll make him walk for you," says Horsetrader. "He ain't sick."

Rodeorider grunts.

Horsetrader opens the pen's gate, an old Kelvinator door. He walks as though each of his steps moved the earth a foot or two. His western boots with high heels and pointed toes give Pig something to think about.

"You see that?" Rodeorider says to Sis.

"What?" says Sis.

"Goddamn!" says Horsetrader.

Pig walks around the pen a few times, flapping his ears, limping a little bit. Rodeorider perks up, chewing now with his mouth open. I look close, but I don't see anything. Earth, touched here and there with soot, looks like brown bread spotted with mold.

"He's got a rupture," says Rodeorider, pointing a courtroom finger, "right there on that hind ham."

Horsetrader lifts Pig's hind leg and looks at the bulging sac that starts on the lower belly and runs down to the ham. It looks like a woman's bathing cap.

"Naw," says Horsetrader.

"Some pig," says Rodeorider.

Horsetrader looks insulted, but I know better. He's just thinking. He's got a ruddy face with a long, broad nose like a plasterer's pointed trowel. Wears black jeans and a black hat. Son of a bitch. Sis wrings her hands: she wants that pig. Horsetrader rolls a cigarette and licks it with his pointed tongue. Rodeorider's so pleased about that rupture, so pleased he's going to be able to bargain with a man like Horsetrader, he's going to buy that pig. And I know something about Horsetrader's style, too: he wouldn't even try to sell something unless it were properly flawed.

"I won't deliver him," says Horsetrader.

"Delivering," says Rodeorider. "What's this about delivering?"

Horsetrader shrugs, pushes his wad farther into the hole.

"He costs fifteen dollars," says Horsetrader, spitting into the pen.

I shoot pebbles, marble-style, against Pig's side, but Horsetrader looks at me once, and I stop.

Rodeorider's never more than two minutes away

from Police Special. He shows it, too, when he tries to laugh: slack-jawed chuckle cut short by chewing. Muscles throb near his temple.

"Let's go," I say, looking at Horsetrader. He smiles, slaps me on the back, squeezes the muscle between my neck and shoulder so hard I can feel it in my eyes, but I don't make a sound. He understands. It was a joke, that's all. About Rodeorider. We both know he's not leaving.

"Shut up," says Rodeorider.

Sis kicks a stone. She's fifteen, one year older than me. She lives in a house with a big yard on a hill in the middle of Hollywood. Like I do. On Horsetrader's porch Oklahoma Kids stop their game of wire, tin, and sticks.

"If I delivered him," says Horsetrader, his eye snapping once toward his children, "which I won't, it'd be five dollars."

Oklahoma Kids listen, memorize gestures.

"But you ain't delivering him," says Rodeorider.

"And you're saving five dollars," says Horsetrader, beginning to smile.

I can feel the pale stare of Oklahoma Kids. Tea-colored eyes. There are three boys and a girl, all of them serious, drawn to their heritage. Abruptly the youngest boy spits into the sooty yard and turns into the house.

Rodeorider steps into the pen and lifts that hind ham.

"I seen it," says Horsetrader, gazing off toward the steam plant. "Little blemish."

"Well . . . ?"

"Some people might be squeamish about a blemish," says Horsetrader with gruff disbelief.

On the porch pale eyes widen.

"That's a five-dollar blemish," says Horsetrader. "Okay?"

Rodeorider grunts and says, "Shit."

In the back lot near the steam plant's fence a burro begins to bray. *Honk! Honk!* I shoot a pebble into a puddle of piss and rainwater near Pig, but Horsetrader looks at me again and I stop. That's some stare for a man with only one eye, I think.

"So," says Horsetrader a little sadly, "he's a ten-dollar pig now."

He looks into the pen as though Pig had been caught at some porky five-dollar sin, some unnatural act. Rodeorider keeps chewing his aspirin gum, looking quickly from Horsetrader to the pen. Luminescent steam escapes from pipes at the end of the back lot.

"But look here," says Horsetrader, "you saved ten dollars already. Five for the delivering and five off the price of the pig."

Sis whispers to me, "He's going to have to count on his fingers soon." She smiles at Rodeorider, but he pretends he doesn't see her.

"Looks to me," says Horsetrader, "like you're getting a free pig."

Sis elbows Rodeorider in the ribs, and he blushes with anger and embarrassment. Horsetrader leans on the Kelvinator door. In his back lot, near the burro, there's a small house trailer, shaped like a drop of water. But it's up on blocks, stumpy axles protruding from the wheel wells, its plywood sides curling from the seams. Distant license plates: Utah, Texas, Oklahoma. Horsetrader's wreck, run aground in his back lot. His eye lingers there, and I think of country girls stopping short at the sound of creaking springs, the thought of a narrow bed.

"Well?" says Horsetrader, looking toward his children.

Rodeorider doesn't know what to do, so he bumps into me and says, "Get out of my way, Niles. What the fuck's wrong with you?"

Sis and I jump back, but Horsetrader just leans on the Kelvinator door. "Put him right in that purple Chevrolet of yours," he says.

Rodeorider hunts for time, chews his aspirin gum slowly. Something from the steam plant makes the air sting a little. Screen door near the end of the porch opens quickly and Oklahoma Kid, the youngest son, runs through it. Before it closes I see Horsetrader's wife, a heavy woman dressed in her underwear and high-heeled shoes: pushed-up breasts, a fan of pale hair through worn cotton.

"Pa," says Oklahoma Kid into the damp yard, "don't sell that pig. Man on the telephone wants him."

Brothers and sister still line the porch, gazing into the yard.

"Says he's putting on a play. Says he needs a pig for it."

Oklahoma Kid spits into the yard, then wipes his lips with the back of his hand. A little smoke from the pale wife's cigarette drifts through the screen door.

"He's calling long distance, Pa. I can hear him putting quarters in the slot. Over in Downey somewhere, he's calling from."

"Looks like it's a rising market, don't it?" says Horsetrader, staring down at Pig.

Oklahoma Kids don't even blink. They've got their hands up on the porch rail as though waiting for the inspection. I know what's happening, though: Horsetrader's going to buy his youngest son a Mars bar tonight. Rodeorider's just thinking about that pig onstage.

"Tell him to get lost," Rodeorider says over his shoulder, but Oklahoma Kid still stands next to the door, and Horsetrader just stares into the pen, ignoring the money, the ten-dollar bill, that Rodeorider offers him. If a look could blind a man, Sis's would, that's sure. Once she caught Rodeorider arranging his money, putting one bill on top of another so that George Washington was always face up, all nice and neat, and she looked at him like she's looking at him now. For being such a fool. But that's why she'll want to do something to him in that Chevrolet on the way home. Not in front of your little brother, Rodeorider will say, chewing his aspirin gum. But they're wrong: I don't care what they do.

"Here," says Rodeorider.

Black birds fly through a billow of steam.

"Seems like a shame," says Horsetrader, "to let the phone company get all those quarters he's putting into the slot."

But he takes it, takes it the way you take a receipt for something you didn't really want to buy.

"How's that, girlie?" he says to Sis.

"All right." But then she sees me smiling and says, "Shut up, Niles."

"Pa?"

"You tell that man over in Downey," says Horsetrader, "you tell him it's too late. Pig's sold."

On the porch Oklahoma Kids turn back to their quiet, sullen games. Youngest son swings the kitchen door open, and I see Horsetrader's wife, her flesh as pale as her worn underwear.

"You got a rope," asks Rodeorider, "or is that extra?"

Steam plant looks like a ship that's not quite built yet: dockyard supports surround its checked smokestack. Up and down the road I see the arms of telephone poles, the dark wires looping from one to another.

Across the street there's a house and it's got telephone wires leading to it, but there aren't any wires leading to Horsetrader's house. Youngest son, when he comes back onto the porch, looks at me, shrugs, and spits modestly into the yard.

You tell that man in Downey, I think, you tell him.

"No," says Horsetrader. "I got a rope."

Rodeorider slaps Chevrolet into reverse and slides it up to the pen's Kelvinator door. Tires leave a lacy pattern in the damp earth. Rodeorider's a hard-driving man: even if he's got to move Chevrolet only twenty feet he's doing twenty miles an hour when he gets there.

Horsetrader brings a piece of rope from the barn. In his back pocket he's got a chipped, worn stick, about two feet long.

"Stop pissing around, Niles," says Rodeorider, "and get on in here."

Horsetrader lights another cigarette. Jesus, can he roll them tight, just like a Camel.

In the pen Rodeorider and I leave smooth, shiny places in the mud when we slip.

"Now, don't you worry, girlie," says Horsetrader to Sis, "that's the nicest, gentlest pig I've ever seen."

Come on, I think, going to put you in the Chevrolet. Flies pick through bits of straw and soot on Pig's back, and a couple buzz around his head, like pilot fish. What the hell, I think, giving him a kick. What the hell. Pig pushes toward me a little, as though he enjoyed it, and flies just ride his back. Lazy flies: must have caught something from Pig. Rodeorider snaps his gum, listens to the watery metabolism of his mind, a trickle of thoughts that's as close as he gets to thinking. Won't be long now, I think. Rodeorider's pupils are the size of dimes.

"Can't hurt a pig," says Horsetrader.

Rodeorider takes two slow steps, says, "All right, porkchop, honey, you just take it easy," and kicks Pig right in the snout, on that coin slot nose. And then Pig's running, with Rodeorider after him, using that rope like a whip. "Blue ball son of a bitch," says Rodeorider. I'm flying through the air, screaming, "Pig, pig, pig," trying to run him into the corner between the barn and the side of the pen. Pig spins there, looking surly as hell, curling his lip, showing his fat tongue and yellow teeth. Rodeorider kicks Pig in the snout, ties the rope around Pig's neck. But Pig takes off again, running around the pen, with Rodeorider hanging onto the rope. That man's crazy, I think, got a pig on a leash. And there's not much Rodeorider can do because Pig's smart enough to stay pretty close to the pen's center.

Horsetrader pushes his wad back and flips his cigarette butt at Pig.

I grab a post and put out a hand, thinking, Jesus, this ain't going to hold. Rodeorider grabs my arm as he comes around. Horsetrader's looking mean, and I know it's got nothing to do with style. Post begins to lift out of the ground, and the side of the pen leans over some.

"He was going to do the talking," I say, "he was going to bargain. . . ."

Horsetrader comes through the Kelvinator door, takes the stick from his back pocket, and uses it to wind the loop around Pig's neck. Looks like Pig's wearing a tourniquet.

"You got to wheeze him, boy," says Horsetrader to me, "you see that?"

I nod, pleased that he showed me something. Pig stands still as a photograph.

"Here, boy," says Horsetrader, "you hang on to this."

We drag Pig across the pen, leaving a smooth, shiny

wake, and throw him into the trunk of the Chevrolet, after swinging him back and forth like a body in a sheet. He bounces once on a chrome upright, begins to squirm, but I take up a half notch with the stick, and he stops that. He lands with a porky thud, his legs still hanging over the bumper. Grayish bag quivers. Rodeorider touches it and Pig flinches, even though he's wheezed down pretty tight.

"He's got to go in catty corner," says Horsetrader.

I pull his head in behind the spare tire.

"Some pig catchers," says Horsetrader. "Couple of minutes more and you'd have pulled my pen down. Look at that." He points to the post and side of the pen. "Shit."

Oklahoma Kids on the porch play their games, not bothering to look at us. Their bits of wire, wood, and glass seem dignified, valuable. Olive trees line the road in front of the house, and I can smell their muskiness. A caravan of house trailers, like segments of aluminum fuselage, move toward the desert. Horsetrader's eye snaps from the back lot, his wreck, to the road. The socket filled with cotton looks like an eye carved by a Greek sculptor.

"Jesus," says Sis to me, "do you stink."

Like a hangman at the trap Rodeorider closes the trunk lid slowly and quietly to show he's not angry, but I know he's thinking: Pig flinched, Police Special.

"You're not getting into my car with that shit all over you," says Rodeorider.

"Maybe I could use his phone," I say, pointing to Horsetrader, "and have someone pick me up."

Horsetrader smiles and says, "Paper's next to the barn."

Pig rustles around in the trunk, trying to get comfortable. From the pile of throw-away advertisers I take a few sheets and spread them over Rodeorider's cowhide seats so I can sit on them. Sis climbs into the Chevrolet, into the front seat, and I see one of her beautiful hands, blood, clear fluid, and scabs: melted rubies, diamonds, an alchemist's crust.

"Thanks for the help," says Rodeorider, stabbing at the dashboard a few times before he gets the key into the ignition. Compression's about gone: Chevrolet starts as easily as a rocking chair.

" 'Snothing," says Horsetrader. "You just have a good time getting him out."

Horsetrader pushes his wad back. I hear Pig bumping around, getting acquainted with spare tire and tools as Rodeorider slides Chevrolet onto the road.

Rodeorider's advice: you got to think of two lines, each one running from an ear to the eye on the opposite side. And where they cross, that's where you got to put it.

You hear me, Niles?

Police Special's so heavy it looks like Rodeorider's got a brick in his jacket pocket.

Rodeorider prays for a wind-broken horse, a rabid dog, a stray cat or two, settles every now and then for a Dr Pepper sign.

Don't ever drink that shit, says Rodeorider, shooting out of the window of the Chevrolet.

I know a sign that looks like a grater.

Our yard has three terraces, and on the last one there's a couple of rabbit hutches, a doghouse and our dog, a goat, a small pond with a couple of mallard ducks in it. Pig's there, too, tied to a tree, wheezed tight, because he's run around the trunk so many times.

"You son of a bitch," says Sis as she runs from the house.

"Get out of the way," says Rodeorider.

Police Special makes the air howl, fills my ears with a gyroscopic ringing, one that changes pitch as I turn my head. Pig blinks, then dances on his back, legs rigid, neck rigid, at least what's left of it anyway, but there isn't much of that. You can see where the bullet came out, except it looks more like it was a bowling ball. Grayish bag on the lower stomach and ham bounces, too. Blood trickles away from him like a caravan of red ants. Confusion sets in: palsied legs run in all directions, awed by slippery sky, the unctuous leaves against it.

"You stupid ass," says Sis.

"Lemme alone," says Rodeorider.

Blood blows into the air, then falls into Pig's neck, the quickened, rasping hole.

"Well," says Sis, "why don't you do it again?"

"He can't use it," says Rodeorider. "That's just throes."

"You'll be sorry," says Sis.

"No I won't," says Rodeorider.

He's right, too. Sis'll do something nice for him. In that Chevrolet.

Rodeorider and I drag Pig to the next terrace, where there's a clothesline made of heavy-gauge pipe. Hind legs make running movements in the air. Behind us, on the path, it looks as though a running garden hose had been dragged over the earth.

"Goddamn," says Rodeorider. "Man wants a pig for a play. What kind of play do you think that is, Niles?"

"I don't know," I say, but I do. One that stars a Rodeorider.

Sis puts her foot into the rusty stain on the path, the curdled dirt.

"You're even more stupid than your father," says Sis to Rodeorider.

"Shit," says Rodeorider, still thinking about that play, but I step back a few feet, not wanting to take any chances.

Sunbather's yard is the next one over, beyond the hedge and wall. I've watched from the bushes: shiny curve of breast, brown belly and thighs, dark hair between her legs. Sunbather's got a skinny husband, and he ain't happy. He scans the sky, curses private planes and police helicopters, coffee-breaking telephone men crucified on their poles. Sunbather always walks like she's naked.

In about a year, I think, looking toward her yard. I don't care about skinny husband.

"God," says Sis, her voice filled with adhesive contempt.

Rodeorider chuckles, grins.

"God," says Sis.

Rodeorider puts the snub nose of Police Special into my ear.

"How about you, Niles?" he says. "You want some, too?"

Police Special's got a warm nose. Rodeorider moves it lightly against the skin and cartilage, lets his hand shake, pulls back the woodpecker hammer.

"I can't use it," I say.

I have a good smile.

Rodeorider snaps his gum, chuckles, taps the barrel on my head.

"Maybe," says Rodeorider with his jaws working, "some other time."

"Don't act crazy," says Sis.

We're slow-motion people. Rodeorider backs away from me the way he would from a balanced coin, a cardhouse. I match his sluggishness with my own until his arm, with Police Special at the end, hangs straight down, as though it were broken.

"Stop it," says Sis.

"Lemme alone," says Rodeorider, but he drops Police Special into his pocket, and begins to sing, quietly, while looking down at Pig. *"My bucket's got a hole in it, don't work no more . . ."*

Sis looks at Rodeorider's weighted pocket, thinking about Police Special. Rodeorider practices fast-draw: Wyatt Earp banging away at Lucky Lager bottles. He hasn't got enough sense to keep all his fingers and toes on, says Sis to me. You can hardly notice Rodeorider's limp now.

I tie the rope to Pig's hind feet, throw the end of it over the small yardarm of the clothesline pole, and hoist him up. I think of Burned setting sail with sheets on washday. Blood drips to the earth with a pulselike cadence, as though out of habit.

"It's a good thing Mother and Father aren't home," says Sis. She means Burned and Hawkeye. Burned still has marks from the last time, from the glass.

"That pig sure can bleed, can't he?" I say to Rodeorider.

"I think I'll just watch," says Sis after she brings from the kitchen a bucket filled with some knives and a hacksaw.

I pierce the belly, feel a puff of damp air on my hands. Hide opens like a man's coat, reveals lapels of fat, membranous shirt taut with coiled works. I cut a tube, and something that's not quite shit yet falls out.

"Don't cut yourself," says Sis, pulling up an aluminum-and-plastic chair. "You can die if you cut yourself."

I carry a tube on a carving fork to the slope below the last terrace where there's nothing except broom and brush. On the path blood mud pulls at my shoes. Tube twirls slowly in the air, small bits from the open ends splattering against the sky. Through the trees I see Rodeorider's arm, with the knife at the end of it, rising and falling, rising and falling, passion-murder style.

"Fucking dull knife," says Rodeorider.

I cut open kidneys, finger seashell half sections.

"See?" I say to Sis. "See?"

She looks at the dismantled bits around her feet, the soft kidney I drop into her lap. Someone, in another yard, turns on a sprinkler, a Rain Bird, and I can hear its watery stutter.

"Don't play around," she says to me, tossing the kidney into a cardboard box beneath Pig.

Rodeorider takes another turn, puts his hand inside, and says, "It's warm. If you're freezing to death you climb inside an animal. That's what you do."

Pig's got a lead-colored eye, tinted by Police Special. I run a finger across its cool surface, respectfully press the globe. Rodeorider slits a spongy lung.

"Alveoli," he says without interest and turns back to the clothesline, knife in hand. He strikes too hard: a metallic fin appears on Pig's back. I slit the heart, the white ridges around the top, push fingers into holes, feel valves soft as clover. Rodeorider works the saw.

"That's a baby," he says.

He picks the head out of the box, holds it above his own, and runs beneath the clothesline.

"Hoot! Hoot!"

He stops beside me, pushes the snout against my ear.

"Hoot!"

Sis isn't impressed.

"That's not the right sound," she says.

Rodeorider takes a few charges at her, paws the ground with one foot, pulls Pig's lips into a silly grin.

"Hoot!"

"Shut up," says Sis.

"What's wrong with those hands, girlie?" he says.

I carry the full box to the hill, but the cardboard bottom, soaked with blood and juices, gives way, and torn, brightly colored organs fall down my legs and onto my shoes. Rabbits push their noses to the wire of their hutches, sniff the air. I kick and shuffle along, pushing the pile ahead of me, then at the edge of the hill use the fork to toss the pieces away. They spin gracefully, rustle as they settle into broom. Head rolls down the hill like a stone, makes the brush crackle.

Sis turns on the flood lamps.

I climb through the bushes next to the terrace, pass the Styrofoam fountain, and see Rodeorider dipping one of Pig's legs into a washtub filled with scalding water. Steam ghosts caress his arms, chest, and face. The rib cage rests behind Rodeorider on the aluminum chaise longue.

"Hot water!" says Rodeorider.

I crawl away, as quiet as an Indian. Every dog in the neighborhood's going to be on that hill tonight, I think. But ours will get first choice, the finest bits.

"Why don't you speak in whole sentences?" says Sis, standing in the kitchen door. There are large kettles of water on the stove.

"Lemme alone," says Rodeorider.

Blood on my face dries and cracks. I climb in the brush, hiss, chant, claw the dirt, always careful about the noise I make. Shadows, long, thickening like baseball bats, move through the trees as Hawkeye and Burned walk in front of the flood lamps.

"Where's that son of mine?" says Hawkeye.

"Niles!" calls Burned.

What are you doing in my house? Tell me! She

dances. Chemical music. I want to dance with the girl with the hole in her stocking, with the hole in her stocking . . . Oh, I . . . Who are you and what are you doing in my house? Get out! She wobbles on high heels. It's your son, Niles. Ask me another.

"Niles!"

Whiz Kid, Answerman. Niles. X-ray eyes, radio ears. My shadow falls across the yard.

Burned screams when she sees me. Hawkeye turns.

"How could you, Niles," she says, her hand just beneath her breasts. "How could you frighten me like that?"

On the picnic table Sis wraps pieces of Pig in wax paper.

"You know I'll be sick tonight," says Burned.

Sis looks at me angrily, because she can't stand it either, the noise we hear later, much later, when Burned falls, bounces, muscles rigid, quivering, frightened by what she sees: clocks with teeth, an orchestra of cockroaches blowing notes of skin, screaming suns, walking nerves dressed in tails and spats.

Hawkeye kneels over her, exposing the soles of his shoes, the bits of metal stuck in them from the floor of the airplane factory where he works. They look like bits of shrapnel. Sis lights incense in her room and begins to chant. Hari, hari, hari . . . I bite my tongue until it bleeds, pleased with the salty taste.

Rodeorider and I sit in his Chevrolet, parked around the corner from our house where Hawkeye and Burned can't see it. Rodeorider broods.

He has a gun, says Burned. He brings animals here.

Hawkeye takes the television apart, spreads the bits around him on the floor. Capacitors, resistors, tubes, colored, spaghetti-like wire.

He shot an animal here, says Burned to Sis, and, anyway, what do you do in that Chevrolet?

Nothing, says Sis.

I saw those cartoons you drew, says Burned, of a man. Of his privates.

Hawkeye looks up from a stripped resistor, and says, Don't see him again.

Rodeorider broods some more, bites on an unlit rum-soaked crook, thinks of bucking horses, riding to the whistle, prize money.

Sis carefully examines the windows and the screens in her room, sees how quietly she can open them. Rodeorider and I wait for her to crash out.

Out of curiosity, I say, "He didn't have a telephone."

"Who's that?" says Rodeorider absently. "Who doesn't have a phone?"

"The man you bought the pig from."

After a while it takes: Rodeorider slips a piece of aspirin gum into his mouth.

"How do you know?" he asks slowly, as though he had a wax tongue.

"Telephone takes wires," I say. "He didn't have any."

One thing Chevrolet's got left is pistons. You can hear their air-show whine as Rodeorider takes off. One thing about Rodeorider: he can swear. "Cock-sucking blue ball son of a bitch," says Rodeorider. When we come to the first stoplight, he doesn't even bother to slow down. He just leans on the horn and sticks his middle finger into the air.

"Load it," he says.

I break open Police Special's metal belly, but I see it's already filled. Rodeorider blows air raid tunes on the horn, screams at drivers on the freeway.

"Gimme that," he says.

Dust from the road blows across the yard, but when

it's gone, I see Horsetrader standing there as though he'd been dropped by the dust itself. Rodeorider doesn't wait to shut off the engine, close the door, or even for Chevrolet to stop. He's out in the yard, with a shooting-range stance, Police Special in his hand.

"What's the problem?" says Horsetrader.

"You ain't got a telephone," says Rodeorider.

"That's as good a reason as any," says Horsetrader, pushing his wad back, "to shoot a man."

"That's what I think," says Rodeorider, pulling back the hammer.

"Maybe a refund," says Horsetrader.

"Pig's already dead," I say. "In the freezer. You got a freezer?"

Pale wife brings a chair onto the porch, sits in weak sunlight and damp air. She drinks from a bottle of cherry pop and smokes a mentholated cigarette. Oklahoma Kids whine behind the screen door.

"Nope," says Horsetrader a little sadly. "That's something I haven't got."

"No refund," says Rodeorider.

Twice condemned: no telephone, no freezer. Wad of cotton in his eye. I know something else, though: if he had the money for a glass eye, he'd get a clear one, like a small crystal ball. But he makes do with wad of cotton.

Steam plant clicks: damp, milky fluff floats over the yard. Beyond the plant I can see the substation, caged electric animals, glass feelers and horns, can hear a sidereal hum. Insulators look like they've been cast from melted Coke bottles.

Horsetrader sees it, too: Police Special's pretty heavy, and Rodeorider's getting tired of drawing a bead on Horsetrader's middle button. His arm begins to wave up and down like a railroad signal. Rodeorider's angry because he can't control it, because he knows now that he should have climbed out of Chevrolet, walked to the porch and shot Horsetrader, if he was going to do it at all. And he's angrier still when he realizes he's got a ten-dollar credit and only one place to shop.

"That," says Horsetrader, pointing to his back lot, "is a thirty-dollar burro."

"No it ain't," says Rodeorider.

"I guess not," says Horsetrader, eyeing Police Special.

"Looks more like twenty," says Rodeorider.

Burro stands next to the house trailer, nuzzling damp earth, trying to find something to eat. Skinny burro. Beneath his mangy hide you can see xylophone ribs.

"All things considered," says Horsetrader.

And just like that I'm leading Burro through the gate of the back lot. Rodeorider's already gone in Chevrolet, up the road about a mile where he and Sis board their horses. Horsetrader holds two ten-dollar bills between his thumb and finger.

Pale wife finishes her cherry pop and throws the bottle into the yard. "Always damp around here," she says, hugging her shoulders.

Horsetrader shrugs, looks toward the steam plant. I lead Burro, aware of his four-footed gait, the movement of his head and thinly swaying back, four snapping ankles. I lead him under the olive trees.

"I was just curious," I say, stopping, turning toward the yard again.

" 'Snothing," says Horsetrader.

House trailers, ribbed, seamed, riveted, some of them large enough to be hauled by trucks, move slowly up the road: it's the season for them. Horsetrader watches with a cataloguer's eye: ten rooms, a skylight, wall-to-wall carpeting, a tiled bath, hot-water heater. I lead Burro among the wide-load signs, the shreds of red cloth, extra reflectors.

"Turn him out with our horses," says Rodeorider, pointing with Police Special to the electric fence, two naked wires that surround the lot. He shoots at beer cans.

"Got a good deal that time," he says.

Beer cans explode, bloom, flash in weak sunlight.

That fence is an attraction, too. Rodeorider and those who live in houses nearby, the remnants of farms and orange groves, sit in the shade, waiting for a bird to land on a wire. Sometimes a bird will reach over to a post to scratch its beak. That grounds a bird. Sometimes you'll have to pry them off the wire, their claws will be wrapped around it so tight. Everyone likes it better when they just fall off, dead.

"We'll take that burro to the auction," I say to Rodeorider.

"You sure you don't want him, Niles?" says Rodeorider as we lead Burro into the horse trailer hitched to the back of Chevrolet.

The auction itself is comprised of a large room, like a medical school surgery, tiered with seats, illuminated by buzzing neon. On both sides of it there are rows of stalls, their slats gnawed into wavy, convoluted patterns. Plains Cowboys stand next to the stalls, drinking out of pint bottles, their eyes filled with quiet contempt for lames, those who take a stance of expertise, who look into mouths, lift hoofs, speak of bowed tendons. There's a rank smell of boiled carrion and crushed bone, the stench of cooking dog food, from the factory that's about a hundred yards or so from the auction.

Plains Cowboys are decked out: hand-tooled belts and boots, clean jeans, sun-bleached to an initiate's

color. Everyone has a wallet on a silver chain. I wander
by the stalls, aware of the humid, manured atmosphere,
the nervous shifting of animals under examination. I
buy a tamale, wrapped in corn husks, dig through piles
of tack, hackamores, cavalry saddles and bits, saddles
from Mexico with wooden trees.

"There'll be a good show," says Rodeorider, gesturing toward the Plains Cowboys.

He's right, too.

Auctioneer begins his amplified stutter. A redhead
Plains Cowboy, his grin changed by his pint, leads a
plains horse into the ring beneath the tiers of seats. But
no one bids.

"Som'bitch," says Plains Cowboy. "He's gentle
enough."

He drops onto all fours, crawls between front legs,
under the belly, tries to lift Plains Horse, moves between the hind legs. Plains Horse kicks him in the head,
on the face, at the top of the brow. Laughing friends
drag him to one of the stalls.

"He ain't dead," says one.

The auctioneer, a crosscountry judge dressed in a
white shirt, bow tie, and suspenders, a man who could
preside at any lynching, says, "You seen the show. It's
time to buy."

I wait Burro's turn, listen to the auction at work, time
being cut into dollars and cents.

"He'll bring in thirty dollars," says Rodeorider.

"They're not bidding much," I say.

"He'll bring thirty," says Rodeorider.

The auctioneer's assistant, the judge's bailiff, tells us
it's Burro's turn. We run him down the space between
the stalls into the ring, where he stands with dropping
ears, confused by people, neon, static.

"Five five five who'll give me five?"

Five, I hear five. I see a long arm gesture from the crowd. Son of a bitch, I think. I know better than to tell Rodeorider.

"Seven seven seven fifty."

Someone, off to my right, gives seven fifty. But the long arm strikes again, makes it an even ten. I move through the crowd to make sure, and then I see him, the long nose, black jeans and boots, a new shirt for the occasion, the wad of cotton in his eye: Horsetrader.

"I got ten ten I got ten last call I got ten."

"How you doing, boy?" says Horsetrader.

"Okay," I say, a little shyly.

"That's good," says Horsetrader. "Glad to hear it."

I begin to walk through the crowd back toward Rodeorider, but I feel Horsetrader's hand on my shoulder, and hear him say, "Why don't you just stay here for a minute or two. Until things are settled."

"Done. Sold. Ten dollars. To the one-eyed man."

I can't see Rodeorider, but I know his head rips around, trying to see Horsetrader. Time to start walking home, I think, time maybe just to leave. But at the clerk's table, where Rodeorider receives eight fifty (ten dollars less auction's commission), he just smiles at Horsetrader, and says, "Good to see you, good to see you," the cords showing in his neck all the time, smiling, smiling, taking his eight dollars and fifty cents and walking straight through the crowd, out the door, to the liquor store across the street where he can buy himself a pint.

Horsetrader turns back to the auction, buys himself a goat, a wire box full of rabbits, a cow, and an old cavalry horse with its serial number branded into its neck.

"That," says Horsetrader, pointing to the horse, "is a museum piece. But he's big enough."

He pushes his wad back, puts a gaudy orange-and-magenta halter around Cavalry Horse's neck.

"You wait here," he says to me.

He leads the horse through the chutes and gates behind the auction, across the paved parking lot to the factory, a scarred horizon, sheets of corrugated metal, towers, smokestacks, bare bulbs, cataracted windows, barbed-wire gardens. Behind me, in one of the stalls, sits Plains Cowboy, blood running from his hair like sweat.

Man's got to know weight, says Horsetrader. Now I'm going to make ten dollars just walking across that parking lot. He's a fifteen-dollar horse on the hoof, but he's a twenty-five-dollar horse by the pound. They, he says, pointing a thumb toward the factory, pay by the pound.

Plains Cowboy opens a fresh pint, looks mournfully at the pile of dry manure he sits on, checks his arms, belly, ribs, legs, winces when he touches his scalp.

"Got kicked in the head," he says with spirited disbelief, "and I was going to a real L.A. cathouse. Som'bitch."

He says L.A. like "El Lay," as though it were part of a chain store.

Horsetrader returns with the empty halter.

Horsetrader's Dodge has long, sharp fins, extra taillights, and a steering wheel that's been cut down so it looks like an airplane's controls. Dodge is filled with old advertisers, food wrappers, beer cans and pop bottles, and smells inside like manure and hay. The glove box, which won't close, is filled with receipts, most of them written on schoolboy's notepaper. Hitched to the rear bumper is Horsetrader's trailer. Its back door has been kicked off a couple of times, but Horsetrader's patched things up with a piece of plywood that must have been at one time part of a fence around a new building. Torn

posters, half a starlet, a politician's smile, and a real
estate sign are still on it. Over the metal canopy of the
trailer hang shreds of canvas, like triangular flags. We
load Burro and the cow into the trailer, put the goat and
the rabbits in the back seat of the Dodge.

"One-eyed man ain't supposed to drive," says Horsetrader. "Some shit about depth perception. But I know
how big things are supposed to be."

I nod.

"You take it easy now," says Horsetrader, pulling out
of the parking lot.

On the freeway Rodeorider drinks his second pint,
sings a song about a dog.

There are burglaries in our neighborhood.

"Some of my tools are missing," says Hawkeye.

He frowns, rummages around in the garage, takes a careful inventory.

"A screwdriver, a hammer, and a chisel."

At night I pry open the window of a house I know to be empty, then slip quietly inside. It's a large house, sprawling around the point of a hill. I make a snack in the kitchen, prowl through the rooms, looking into private places for old love letters, stock, deeds, a birth certificate: paper edged with printed lace, intricate designs, validated with an inked footprint. I'm angry when I find a locked wall safe. Woman's underwear, flesh-scented, small bottles in the medicine cabinet, bank statements, secrets. In the library there are good books and a deep, soft couch. I read for a while, nap, and then leave, carefully arranging things as I found them.

* * *

Hawkeye sits on the living room floor, surrounded by bits of television. He takes a drink of Ripple, then makes a smoky stab with his soldering gun. He reads a resistor's color scheme, worries about capacitors, amplifying tubes.

"Ohms," he says to himself.

Blood-rare turkey cooks in the oven. Sis hides in her room.

"Ohms."

Burned fingers a mark above her brow, smiles, balances a Ripple bottle on her knee.

Rare turkey, I think, Ripple wine: Wineskin's coming to dinner.

"Yes, he is," Burned says, "and you be nice to him."

"He lost his job," says Hawkeye, splattering bits of solder on the floor. He waits for them to harden, then clowns, picks the shiny drops from the floor, sticks them on his face.

Wineskin's a repossession man, spends his days snatching TVs, couches, toasters, cars. Especially cars. What the hell, I think, someone's happy: roller derby's on tonight.

Sis stands in front of her mirror examining her naked body, the beautiful eruptions shaped like roses on her skin. When she lies on the bed I gently touch the inflamed ridges, soft, petal-shaped sores. I bring ice from the kitchen, cool the tips of my fingers, then apply them to the rubbery welts.

"What's the verdict?" I ask, meaning Wineskin.

Sis points to a painful spot, then says, "He was repossessing a Cadillac. Up in the hills. But he didn't have the keys, and he didn't want trouble with the people who owned it. And since the Cadillac was unlocked, he thought he'd just climb in and coast it down the hill a little bit. When he got far enough away he was going to call a tow truck."

I trace the rosy pattern. "That wasn't smart," I say.

"He found that out," says Sis.

Cadillac's got power brakes and steering. They work off the ignition.

She begins to dress in her superstitious, halting way. She runs the smooth material of her underwear across her lips before putting any of it on: it brings good luck.

"There was a long piece of street before the first turn," says Sis.

I understand: old Wineskin strains behind the wheel, both of his feet on the power brake that doesn't do any good. Dear God, he thinks, save me now, as Cadillac jumps the curve, prunes the hedge, and slams through the house's wall, right into the bedroom. Cadillac's value decreases. Thank God my bottle didn't break, thinks Wineskin, may His truth be told. He sits in the pile of scrap iron, having a drink or two, looking through the windshield at the woman sitting up in her bed. She doesn't say anything. She just gives him a mean look: it's that part of town.

"Ohm," says Hawkeye.

Burned answers the knock at the door.

"See you got the TV apart again," says Wineskin.

He walks through the living room as though his backbone were a spring. His shoelaces are untied, and one of the lenses in his glasses is cracked. Raw veined jowls.

Hawkeye uses the soldering gun, grunts, then says, "Too bad about your job."

"Got another Ripple, honey?" says Wineskin to Burned.

"Sure do," she says.

Wineskin collapses on the couch, looks at Hawkeye through the empty TV set, tries to tune him in.

"Land of Onan," says Wineskin to me, "you're getting to be a big boy. You know what Onan did?"

Hawkeye looks through the TV at Wineskin, chuckles, and says to him, "Don't give away your family secrets."

Wineskin lives alone in a one-room apartment off Hollywood Boulevard.

"Now, now," says Burned.

We eat blood-rare turkey. Wineskin sings the repossesion song: *"Oh give me a home, where the Cadillacs roam, and the Fords and the Mercuries play. . . ."* He elbows me in the ribs, laughs, blows rare turkey across the table.

Sis looks at her plate, frightened.

"Balance and symmetry," says Wineskin. "I was a valve in the merchandise flow."

"That's right," says Burned.

"Got another Ripple, honey?" asks Wineskin.

"Sure do," says Burned.

The room is quiet, except for the noise Wineskin makes as he takes his bridge from his mouth and sucks the bits of rare turkey from it.

"Land of Onan," he says absently, thinking of the room off Hollywood Boulevard.

He sees me looking at his loving hands. "My brother was a surgeon," he says, pointing a finger at me. "Remember that."

Later, I hear him in the bathroom, retching. I open the door, watch him support himself on the toilet bowl, the porcelain and his hands covered with flecks of rare turkey.

"I used to read you stories," he says, a string of saliva dripping from his lips. He forgets which finger accuses, settles for an open hand. "I used to put you and your sister in that tub."

"I'm sorry," I say.

"Sure you are," he says, confused now, trying to slap the toilet's metal lever. "You always were a good boy."

In the extra room he falls onto the bed, breaking the slats and frame. I turn out the light and close the door.

Cheap fucking bed, I think.

Hawkeye turns on the phonograph, plays it so loud no one can speak. I see him through the TV screen, his lips moving.

"Fidelity," they say.

Burned sits on the couch, every now and then raising her eyebrows, a gesture of confused and hostile resignation that frames unseeing eyes.

I pry open windows, jimmy doors, climb drainpipes to unexposed sections of the houses. Attics are filled with trunks, wedding gowns, uniforms, personal relics, yellowed photographs of ancestors, Indian fighters, stevedores, and tradesmen with waxed mustaches and bowler hats. The cloth and paper is musty, molding, rank. I look for birth certificates, documents, secret plans, run across a pile of checks written over the last twenty years.

In the morning Hawkeye wants to wake me, but he can't call my name. He stands next to my bed, working a metal Halloween cricket.

"Niles," says Sis as I walk into the living room. "Niles!"

I look toward the fireplace where Burned stands, tossing Sis's clothes into the flames. Underwear, dresses, coats.

"You didn't keep your room clean," says Burned.

Sis runs across the room, snatches a dress, tries to stamp out the flames on the hearth.

"That will teach you," says Burned.

Hawkeye has a mirror set up in front of the TV so he can see the screen while he makes adjustments at the back of the set.

"Not sharp enough," he says. "There's still a ghost."

Sis watches the burning clothes, holds in front of her breasts the dress she snatched, puts an arm through an ashen sleeve, through the charred delicacy of the cloth.

"Have to take her apart again," says Hawkeye.

I hear Sis in her room, wailing before her shrine, goldfish and incense, doilies and a photograph of Krishna. At night I bite my lip, watch her skin flower. Halloween Cricket wakes me in the morning. I watch Sis setting traps in her room, a small bit of paper on her brush, a hair set on a bottle of perfume, a dark thread laid across her bureau drawer: she wants to see if anyone enters while she's away.

Hawkeye works the TV like a Chinese puzzle, grumbles over the printed schematic, an ohmmeter, makes plans for the assembly of scattered parts. "That's it," he says approvingly. He watches cartoons, comments on the sharpness of the lines, puts Stravinsky on the phonograph, watches television without the sound.

"Fidelity," says Hawkeye.

I climb through the bushes into a large yard, pass rabbit hutches and a dog that doesn't bark, walk up a dirt path toward the house. Moonlight falls softly over the terrace. Goddamn, I think, standing next to the house, hearing the noise the screwdriver makes in the window's aluminum frame. Goddamn, someone's going to hear that. With a gentle rush the screen falls into the bushes around my legs. There's tape and a glass cutter in my bag: an easy, quiet way to get to the window latch, a shiny brass lever that looks like part of a tuba.

It seems like I'm running even before the light flashes on, down the driveway to the back of the house where Sis stands in the lighted kitchen. She wears her night-gown.

"Niles," she says as I come through the door.

The weighted pillowcase hangs next to my leg.

"Niles," she says, "there's someone trying to break into our house."

Later she comes to my room, touches my head, calls me by a nickname.

"Why are you crying?" she asks.

Hawkeye stands next to my bed, holding in his fist Halloween Cricket, a small black-and-orange bug with a metal tab for guts. Hawkeye's face is severe, just this side of dancing with tics: he's thinking about calling my name, using that bug. His complexion has a medieval cast, the tone and color of an aging portrait.

"There's a detective here to see you," he says.

"I'm awake," I say.

But he can't stop it: Cricket sounds like someone trying to rip a beer can in half.

"Detective's in the living room," he says, with the bug snapping in time to each syllable.

I glance toward the window.

"Nothing doing," says Hawkeye. "I'll wait while you dress."

He notices with some sadness and resentment, too, manliness covering a boy's body, the first lump of mus-cle, a natural threat.

I gotta look out, thinks Hawkeye, the next time I kick
his ass.

"Get a move on," says Hawkeye. "In there."

"I know where it is," I say.

A man with a suicide-ledge expression, a shiny suit,
and greasy hair sits on the couch, smoking a cigarette,
avoiding my eyes. He fiddles with his tieclip, one that's
about as wide as a carving knife.

"You haven't got a thing on me," I say.

"What?" says Tieclip.

Burned comes into the room with her stuttering,
smiling grace.

"I'm clean," I say. "You're wasting your time."

A loony, thinks Tieclip, I got 'em all on this route. He
ignores me and takes from his briefcase his samples of
soap, perfume, brushes, depilatory, the Fuller Brush
man's burden.

"That's just what I needed," says Burned. She buys
more than she needs or wants and says to Hawkeye,
after the brush man leaves, "That's not a funny joke.
He'll gossip to the neighbors."

Hawkeye walks through the house chuckling and
working his bug.

We've got half a family, I think, all of the hate, none of
the love.

"Well, well," says Hawkeye, "it looks like you really
caught it this time."

He looks at the torn flesh, bloodstained skin.

I climb into the gulley beneath the reservoir's sluice
pipe. The gulley is filled with the stinging odor of moss
and frogs, too, hopping green and black blobs, webbed
feet, pouty grins. When I catch one it feels like a cold
heart in my hand. The gulley is lined with ferns and
plants, so many of them it looks as though the reservoir

were leaking green fluid. The sluice pipe is covered
with a gate of iron bars, each about an inch in diameter,
and each ending in a sharp point. The points are buried
in dark silt. Beyond the gate at the end of the pipe
there's a shallow pool, and I can hear frogs croaking
softly there, water from the reservoir dripping into it
with a cadence as regular as a ticking clock. I slide in the
mud like a reptile, stabbing for frogs, then strain at the
gate, hearing the ancient hinges squeak. I prop it open
with a stick. Cold slime pushes through the elbows and
knees of my clothes as I climb toward the pool: a private
place, damp air, aquatic light, holy loneliness. The pool
looks like a watery target, corrugated with concentric
ripples. I squat there for a moment, then slither, on my
back, toward the gate. Blank event, stupidity: I kick the
stick. For a moment I see sky barred by the moving
gate, hear the ancient hinges squeak. A point pierces
the web between chest and arm.

Goddamn stick, I think.

I can feel cold metal in warm flesh, blood running
down my side, knees street-fighting weak. The stain
spreads over my shirt, around the hole in it. I lift the
gate and squirm away, feeling something rip against
the point.

My guts are coming out, I think when I look inside
my shirt. But it's just some curdled, pinkish fat.

"What happened?" says Burned. "Oh, Niles. You
know I'll be sick tonight. Why can't you help out?"

"Well, well," says Hawkeye, "it looks like you really
caught it this time."

In my room I spread a towel on my bed, take off my
shirt and lie down. Hawkeye comes after me, carrying a
new bottle of iodine.

"What is it?" he says.

"Gate spike," I say, "up at the reservoir."

Hawkeye grunts.

"You think there's any dirt in it?" he says.

"I don't know," I say.

He sticks his finger into the wound, searches for a pebble, a bit of moss, a damp shred of wood. His finger comes out the other side, in my armpit. I don't squirm, or blink, but water runs from my eyes.

"How old are you?" says Hawkeye.

Who? Niles? Can you say my name?

"Who?" I say.

"You're old enough to stop this shit," says Hawkeye.

"Who?"

Hawkeye opens the bottle of iodine.

"I'm almost seventeen," I say. "The name's Niles."

Hawkeye blushes, then becomes angry, empties the bottle into the wound.

"Niles," I say.

I walk through milky blindness, the morning fog. The shack is a two-room building made of graying wood, topped by a corrugated tin roof. The windows are covered with rag curtains. It sits on the beach between ocean and highway, protected by a high bluff. I can't see the waves, but I can hear them breaking in the salty fog.

"I need a place to stay," I say to Horse-T.

The shack's first room is filled with limping furniture, a picnic table and two benches stolen from the park, overstuffed chairs bleeding fleece, an Oriental rug thrown over the concrete floor. Horse-T, who's about my age, eighteen maybe, sits on a chair in front of the open icebox, looking for something to eat. His features are rough and uneven, as though he'd been brought into the world with a chain saw and a chisel. He speaks with a farmboy's easy cadence, digs among the heels of bread, half-devoured chicken, drying salami, cans of beer.

"Who are you?" he asks.

"I need a place to stay," I say.

"I don't know you," he says. "Go away."

"I seen you around," I say. At drive-ins, garages, a used-car lot that sells funny cars.

"Good," he says. "Beat it."

On the highway I find a parked car, a Mercury, and climb into the back seat, but it doesn't last long.

"What are you doing in there?"

I open my eyes: bright sun, blue sky, an angry face.

"What are you doing?"

"Trying to sleep," I say, climbing out the door on the other side.

Owner glares at me, sniffs the inside of the car.

On the beach I take off my shirt and shoes, roll the pant legs of my trousers, try to camouflage myself. Men and women lie in the sun, each one slowly turning on an invisible spit. I eat a hamburger out of wax paper, think about catching a gull for dinner.

I see Horse-T in a grocery buying cold wine.

"Look," he says in the parking lot, "it's like a club. Kind of a club."

"Kinda a club," says Lophead. Each word he says is punctuated with a twist of his head. "Exclusive."

"You understand?" says Horse-T.

I understand.

Horse-T mentions a place, and at night I wait there, in a parking lot of a drugstore off Hollywood Boulevard. The sidewalk's filled with limping people, shuffling along, slope-shouldered, cane-propped, on leave from a local retirement house, the street with Saturday-night cars, washed, waxed, and tuned. Couples sit in them like Siamese twins, bound together at the waist. They wait stoically at the stoplight.

"You're Niles, aren't you?"

"Yes," I say, immediately not liking the friendly question, the young man who asked it.

"I'm taking it tonight, too," he says.

He speaks with a simpering camaraderie, points out his new Chevrolet, tells me he's been to London whorehouses. He wears clean clothes.

"You got any money?" I ask.

"What you need it for?"

I point across the street to the deli, the chickens turning on a spit there.

"Going to ransom a bird," I say.

"Sure," he says, giving me five dollars.

In the parking lot I eat the chicken out of its thin wax paper, throw bones at the limpers if they come too close.

"You're pretty hungry," says London Cathouse, watching the way I eat.

I can't help it: I laugh at him. London shows his stupidity, laughs along with me. He's tall, has a face scarred with features, a suspicious expression, little understanding. I steal a dollar of his change.

"Why are you going to take it," I ask, tossing away a chicken bone, "what with that new Chevrolet of yours and all?"

He shrugs and says, "I get lonely."

That's a luxury, I think.

Drugstore's vermilion neon gives London rabbit eyes.

"Look here," he says, by way of explanation, dragging from the trunk of his Chevrolet a large burlap sack and a square five-gallon tin that at one time must have held imported olive oil: a few printed leaves, a branch, happy workers in the groves, antiquated script. The sack smells like it's filled with horseshit.

"I've been pissing in that for a week," says London, pointing to the can.

"Good," I say.

Limpers stare.

"They charge you anything?" I say. "Any kind of fee?"

"Sure," he says. "Fifty bucks."

Horse-T never misses a chance, I think, not one.

A limper stands next to the traffic pole, pushing a button there, stopping traffic so she can get a better look at the couples sitting in the cars.

"This ain't any time for luxuries," I say. "You'll get hurt."

London looks angrily at me, locked into his thick head, hating it so much his eyes bulge. It's going to cost him a lot, I think, to get rid of that fifty bucks.

He sits next to me and says softly, "I know I'm being taken, but what can I do?"

"If you get lonely," I say, "nothing."

He looks at me a little desperately, finally decides I've done him a favor, and says, "Thanks."

The Mercury, a '49, all primered, no grill, looking like a shark, pulls quickly into the parking lot. Cap's driving. He's tall and fat, his skin filled tight as sausage. He smokes a plutocrat's cigar. Tires squeal like a demon's offspring.

"Come on, you dumb bastards," he screams, throwing me the keys, "open up the trunk."

Mercury's full up: I know where we're going to ride. London neatly stows his goods, his can and his sack, into the trunk of the car.

"You ready, Niles?" says Cap as I hand him the keys.

He sees me looking at that cigar.

"For the occasion," he says, pushing its tip against my open hand. It feels like a bite, a hot mouth. Cap watches my lids, waits for one of them to flinch, and says, "We'll see."

Horse-T sits on the other side of the front seat, riding shotgun. He's got a quiet load on. I can see his large eyes, twisted features, broken nose.

"How are you tonight?" I say to him. "You all ready?"

He looks at the limper who's stopping traffic.

"Gonna be some fun," I say. "That's what I heard."

"Tell him to get in the trunk," says Horse-T, leaning easily against the door with his farmboy's slouch. "Tell him to shut up."

"Get in the trunk and shut up," says Cap.

Lophead pulls up in another car, a '51 Dodge, a one-nighter, a favor brought from a junkyard with a gallon of wine. Dodge's throttle is a piece of twine that runs from under the hood to the wind wing on the driver's side. Lophead holds it in his hand as though he were driving a team of horses.

Trunk lid slams shut, chops vermilion neon, the stares of curious limpers.

London and I lie in the trunk's scented darkness, among the sack and can, a spare tire, rags and tools, the two of us curled together like dueling pistols in their case, my shoes under his chin. Angry limpers shout as Cap drives the Mercury between them, over the curb, and into the street. In the tank gasoline makes an artificial sloshing, a sound from a studio lifeboat movie.

"Will they hit us?" asks London.

"Yes," I say absently, listening to the drive shaft, feeling its warmth coming through the floorboards.

"Why are you going to let them," asks London with his desperate anger, "if you're so fucking smart?"

Goddamn, I think, it's earthquake weather, too. During the day there's a silty, heavy sky, a brooding sun. It's not cold but your skin crawls, and then the day shuts

down quickly, surprisingly so, leaving the air cold and
massive. If you're smart you don't wait, but everyone
does, especially me: sitting in bed, straining, hearing
furniture walk to the center of the room, the trees
outside the window collapsing like palace guards.

"Huh?" says London in a weakening, proselytizing
voice.

"Shh," I say, "quiet. Think about something else."

Mercury bucks, slides in a turn, its tires squealing.
Piss smells like rotten grapefruit. Horn blows behind us:
Lophead's Dodge.

"We've got a ways to go," I say, "someplace where
there's no people around."

Mercury begins to climb, then comes to a level place,
the backbone of the ridge.

"Jesus," says London, "I hope they take it easy."

Mercury makes a left turn onto a dirt road: I can
smell dust coming into the trunk. Cap tries to double-
clutch into first gear, but misses the shift, grinds the
gears. I think about protecting myself, my groin and
head, about taking atomic-attack positions, hands
clasped behind neck, knees curled to chin. Mercury
stops short, and then the Dodge, behind us. More dust
rises into the trunk. London makes comforting noises to
himself.

Doors slam. Laughter.

We're out quick, running, too. Horse-T stands behind
the Mercury, holding above his head a branch he's
ripped from a tree, its leaves spreading like an emper-
or's fan against the red sky, the city's gaseous dome. By
the headlights I can see we are in a wide trough, a
shallow depression between two ridges. On one side
there's a house that's being built, and I can see its
woody skeleton, plumber's pipe in naked walls, sawhorses, an outhouse, piles of lumber, a circular saw be-

neath a plastic shroud. A cement mixer, looking like an ancient crusted pot, sits next to a pile of sand. Horse-T's branch moves gracefully, its leaves snapping.

"Oh," says London. "Oh."

But I just keep running until I feel a fist against the side of my face. Lophead stands there, smiling easily. Knees give out: I sit straight down on my haunches. The air smells of fresh wood, damp foundations.

"Where you going, Niles? Where you going?" asks Lophead.

"No place," I say.

Lophead's boots land along my side, in my armpit, at the side of my head. I roll quickly back toward the Mercury. London protests but not for long.

"Shh," someone says to him in a soothing tone.

He nods emphatically, tries to show he's learned something.

"Get that shit out of the car," says Lophead.

Horse-T sweeps London along the ground, using the branch as a broom. I hear a crackling sound in the clump of trees as guests and sleazy dignitaries tear limbs from the trunks.

"Don't rip off all the leaves," says Lophead with a veteran's voice. "They sting."

Enthusiastic guests have branches the size of my forearm. London screams.

"Quiet," someone whispers softly. "Shh."

Guests' women sit on the hood of the Mercury, smoking cigarettes, watching. One has a quiet, sullen beauty: dark long hair, indifferent eyes, moonlight skin. I look up at her, catch her eyes, become pleased that she is bored. She smiles, then looks away.

London looks around wildly, hops up and down in pain, tries not to make a sound.

"Take 'em off," says Lophead.

We drop our clothes into a neat pile.

Lophead's right: the leaves work, but it's the limbs that do unnoticed damage, that numb the opening skin. Penis shrivels because the air is cold. Guests swing slowly, struggle with the branches' bulk, chase London as he runs like a hairless, sloppy dog. Cap puts the tip of his cigar into my ear: eyes water, pain blooms, makes it difficult to breathe. Horse-T watches me in the light from the Mercury, his features strained with recognition.

"Horseshit fight," says Lophead.

I walk clumsily to the sack, listing toward my ear. The girl sits on the hood of the Mercury, one leg drawn up, her chin resting on its knee. She says softly, slightly embarrassed, as I walk by, "My name's Abbey," then walks quickly to the Mercury's door and climbs inside.

London scrambles toward the sack on all fours, not looking ahead or to either side.

"Make a big pile," says Lophead. "You know." He holds his arms as though he were carrying a bushel basket. "Like it was dropped from an elephant."

London uses his arms as a grader.

"You cold, Niles?" says Horse-T.

I can't help it: I'm shivering.

"You cold?"

"I don't feel it," I say.

"We ain't done yet," says Horse-T, becoming angry, recognizing one of his kind. "You son of a bitch," he says, hitting me once, full in the face, hard. "Who do you think you are?"

I find myself staring at leaves, sand, and blood: got hit too hard.

Niles?

Hmm?

"Niles?" says Lophead. "You awake yet?"

"Hmm?"

"That's better," says Lophead.

London busies himself with the pile, getting it just right. Horse-T walks away, toward the house, the sand-pile, where he sits and lights a cigarette.

London has a stupid, hopeful expression, he's made a perfect pile of shit.

"That's nice," says Lophead, stroking London's head. "That's a right nice job."

"Horseshit fight," says Cap, prodding me with his boot. "You get it?"

"You better not lose, Niles," says Cap.

Guests flip on Mercury's spotlight and swing it in our direction. It startles me: teeth chatter. Blood, as warm and fluid as candle wax, runs down arms and legs, drips from the tip of a shaking finger, tickles.

"You understand?" says Cap, gesturing with the cigar between scissor fingers. I wonder if my flesh clung there, at the end of it, if he smoked it. The coal's so hot it's sticky, like the bottom of an ice tray. "You fight him," he says, pointing to London, "there." He points to the pile.

London takes the stance of a TV wrestler, then clowns, snorts, paws the pile, kicking shit backward. Guests stand around us, leaning on their branches like frontiersmen on their rifles. London has a simpering expression, a manikin's smile: he's almost happy.

"Come on," says Cap.

London looks surprised, falls backward, onto the pile, grabbing himself between the legs, screaming. Guest takes a cut at him, but it does no good: he just lies there, his mouth open, trying to breathe. Cap urinates on his head, back, shoulders.

"Quiet now," says Cap. "Just stand up."

Which London does, but crazily, as though he popped out of a box.

"Beat it," I say to him, "go on. They won't stop you."

He looks around, sees it's true.

"No," he says.

"Good," says Cap.

Someone pushes me and then I'm on him, swinging, hitting his head, stomach, pushing the strawlike shit into his mouth, eyes, nose. My knee finds his neck, the bobbing larynx there. He rolls back, and kicks me, catches me just below the breastbone, throws shit, mutters, becomes confused, whispers endearments, is cut down by Cap's branch.

"What's wrong with you?" says a Guest.

London looks at me, flinches under the branch.

"What's wrong with you?"

London finds in the shit the stone he built the pile around, and throws it at me, catching me on the brow, just above the eye. He pounds at the tear in the skin, uses his elbows as thick, short clubs. He makes a mistake, begins to stand, his legs slightly apart, then sits down slowly, holding himself, his mouth open, plainly amazed at what he feels. Cap kicks him beneath the chin. *Clop! Clop!* London caught his tongue. He shakes his head, dribbles blood and saliva on my arm, looks around with an innocent disbelief, stands and half runs, bent at the waist, among the sawhorses, through the skeleton of the house to the bushes on the other side.

"Let him go," says Horse-T. "He's done."

"No he ain't," says Lophead.

I hear London making rustling sounds, digging in the leaves. Lophead walks around the house, listens, cocks his head like a curious dog, reaches into the foliage and pulls London out by one leg, then grabs the other and walks him back, wheelbarrow style. I see London's silvery urine tremble to the ground. Lophead parks him next to me, on a bench of piled lumber. His side is covered with brownish leaves, looks like a dragon's skin.

"Take it easy," I say, putting a hand on his shoulder.

Cap empties London's can over us. The fluid is cold, and it stings in cuts. The rest of them, Guests, run toward us, as though they'd been given a signal, swinging their branches. London takes one look and rolls off the lumber. He stares at me when he gets a chance, tries to rock back and forth, pulls his knees against his thin chest. The leaves sting like vipers' mouths, bite into skin, draw blood. The air is filled with moving clubs.

London kneels and vomits.

"Run," screams Cap, "down the road."

London moves from the bushes, but Cap stops him. We run slowly on the road because the gravel cuts our feet, and the Guests stay with us, swinging their branches scythe-style at our legs. Some of the others, who were left behind, catch up and begin to throw eggs. I see black ovals against red sky. They fall against us with dull, flat sounds. One hits London on the face, at the side of his eye, and it bulges momentarily out of the socket. Between two fingers there's blood mixed with gluey white and broken yolk, a viscous web.

Lophead picks up a two-by-four from a pile of scraps near the house and comes after us. London looks over his shoulder and breaks into a full-gaited run, no longer caring about the gravel. Lophead catches me first, lifts me into the air with one cut of the heavy, damp wood. He holds the two-by-four over his head and swings it straight down, as though he were trying to split a log. He misses, spits at me, then jumps back. Guests stop at the side of the road to gather stones.

Cars follow us as we run. Lophead sits on Mercury's

hood, applying the two-by-four whenever he gets a chance. There's a drainage ditch, filled with water, at the side of the road and I fall into it, settling into the deep mud at the bottom. A stone knocks London down, but Lophead sweeps him into the ditch with me. We shiver in the muddy water, making its surface quiver. It's scaled like armor in Mercury's light.

"Rub it in," I say, dredging mud from the bottom of the ditch and pushing it into hot sores and split skin.

"Tell them to stop it, Niles," says London, "tell them."

I put my head under water, feel its coolness around my face, neck, burning ears: it feels good.

London speaks to his fingertips, whispers to the palms of his hands.

"Wash off," says Horse-T, "there." He points to a bucket and a faucet at the side of the shack. "You ain't coming inside with that shit all over you."

"We got a clean place," says Lophead with a housekeeper's pride.

Pebbles click in receding waves. I draw a bucket of water from the faucet and pour it over my head like a fluid nightshirt. I rub cold lather from a bar of Ivory soap over my chest, legs, and arms until it looks like I'm wearing a suit of white, wet fur. On the other side of the shack Lophead feeds his dog and her pups, Dalmatians, their skins looking like an old sink with some of the porcelain worn off, exposing spots of black metal. In the fog I can hear the eating dogs, busy pups, making the sound of a boiling caldron.

Lophead elbows me in the ribs and says quietly. "Get all cleaned up. We've got something special coming."

Through the rag curtains I see Horse-T turning on the bare bulbs that hang from the ceiling.

"Something special," says Lophead.

He sees my eyes in the light from the shack. "No," he says, "we ain't going to beat you any more. Something special."

"Leave him alone," says Horse-T from the shack. "You get your ass beat, you want to be left alone."

Don't leave me here, says London, plainly stricken. Why are you leaving me here? You hit me.

Horse-T, Lophead, Cap look away, shrug.

Catch us if you can, says Cap, getting into the Mercury.

This is part of it, says London to me, isn't it, Niles?

I shake my head, climb into the back seat of the Mercury. I'm sorry that the girl, Abbey, has already driven off with the rest of them in the Dodge. Lophead, Horse-T, and Cap sit in the front seat.

Niles! screams London.

The Mercury begins to move down the gravel road. London follows, running as well as he can.

I've got more money, he yells, running, straining for enough breath to make himself heard. I've got it in my car.

Cap begins to slow down, looks at Horse-T.

No, says Horse-T, shaking his head. There are limits.

We could use another fifty, says Cap.

No, says Horse-T.

I push cold lather between my legs, feel dried mud there like a rough cast. The shack's roof is made of corrugated metal, rippled with even waves. I rinse a final time, let my teeth chatter freely, then towel with a blanket and put on my clothes. Voices and laughter from the shack melt into the fog. Pups are haunted by splashing water.

"Niles?" says Lophead.

"Just about done," I say. "Yes, sir. Getting all cleaned up."

He laughs. His head bends toward his shoulder as though his neck were broken, moves back and forth in time to his gait or speech, mechanically, as though it were run by gears and tubes, hydraulic blood.

"Hurry up," says Lophead. "We're waiting on you."

"And someone else," says Friend.

Horse-T sits on a lame chair, rocking slowly back and forth. Lophead sits on the floor, drinking from a quart cherry pop bottle, its contents the color of brake fluid. Three others, three Friends, lean against the wall, squat in the corners.

"Where's Cap?" I ask.

"He'll be back," says Horse-T. Horse-T smiles.

"How you feeling?" asks Lophead seriously, with genuine concern.

"Leave him alone," says Horse-T. "You can put your stuff in there." He points to the other room. "That cot's yours."

I put my things in the corner of the room: spoils from the house of Hawkeye and Burned, taken secretly through a jimmied window. Sis saw me, kissed my hand. There are yellow stains on the cot, circular lazy patterns like a snake's skin. I unroll my sleeping bag, hang some clothes on hooks. Home is where the stains are.

Lophead looks out the door. "What if she won't come?" he says.

"She'll come," says Horse-T, "she's got to. Can't live without it."

Lophead laughs, shifts nervously, his head twisting. He has narrow, slanted, almost Oriental eyes, high, knobby cheeks.

"Sure hope she comes soon," he says.

He sees me fingering a sore beneath my shirt. No one has a mirror, but I know there are dark bruises on my face, as though there were soot beneath the skin.

"Hope you washed good, Niles," says Horse-T. "That horseshit can give you one mean infection."

"Oooo, infection," says Lophead. "What's keeping them? Jesus."

"He got an infection once," says Horse-T, pointing a thumb in Lophead's direction.

"Ain't nothing like it," says Lophead with displaced enthusiasm. "Cap's bringing the infection, huh?"

"Something bit him," says Horse-T.

Lophead snorts.

"You want to know how he got bit?" says Horse-T.

"No," I say, "I can figure it out myself."

"Tell him," says Lophead. He looks toward the door.

"His old man dies. Poof, just like that. But the old man's no dummy. He's been betting against himself, so there's five thousand for Lop. Insurance money. Five thousand, right?"

"Right, right," says Lophead. "Lot a money. Suppose to go for my education." His head moves from side to side, pivots on eyes that watch the door.

"Some education," says Lophead.

Horse-T laughs.

"His old lady starts balling this guy. And it turns out he's a chinchilla salesman. You know, everybody's got to have a chinchilla. Right?"

Models stand in full-length coats. I want to reach inside, feel warm skin, a smooth firm belly, smell the musk.

"And while he's balling her he's telling her how much money there is in chinchillas."

"Loads," says Lophead, warming up. "Lots a money."

"You see what's coming?" says Horse-T.

"Too bad," I say.

"For the five grand, Lophead got exactly ten chinchillas, cages included."

"And an instruction manual, and collars. They gotta wear collars or they'll eat their fucking hair off," says Lophead.

Hear-no-evil, see-no-evil Friends sit in the corners, nodding slowly.

"Problem was," says Lophead, "bottom fell out of the market. 'Bout a week after we bought."

"We waited," says Lophead, "we waited for that market to climb. Salesman said it was just a panic, but then he didn't come around any more. And we're getting more chinchillas from the first ten. More cages! More food! Son of a bitch. Got to clean those fucking cages twice a week."

In his hands he holds his works, wrapped in a clean piece of cloth.

"Where are they?" he says, looking toward the door. "Sure are taking their time."

"Maybe she's taking a bath," says Friend.

"She doesn't do that," says Lophead.

"One of them bit me, too," says Lophead after a moment. "Thought I was going to die. Hand puffed up like a Mickey Mouse balloon." He shows us the hand. "One day I took my old man's gun, and I shot every one of those bastards, every one, right in their fucking cages." He smiles: a good job well done.

"What happened to the salesman?" I ask.

"He got into bomb shelters," says Lophead, "right at the end of the boom. He keeps them in a vacant lot over in Culver City. Talks about the Chinese a lot." He chuckles absently, as though out of habit.

Mercury turns from the gravel road onto the sand, its

tires hissing. Engine dies, and then the lights. Our shadows evaporate from the wall. I can hear quiet coaxing
sounds outside.

"Took him long enough," says Lophead. He digs
through a cardboard box in a corner, finds what he's
looking for, a swollen manila envelope, and puts it on
the picnic table. "She usually likes that," he says. He
moves around the room, straightening things, blowing
dust off the top of the icebox, moving chairs, clearing a
place in the center of the room.

Cap walks through the door.

"Well," he says, "if it ain't Mr. Niles Cabro."

She follows Cap.

"Come on in, sweetheart," he says. "You know everybody."

She hesitates at the door, light-shy, apprehensive.
One eye is a little larger than the other. Thin blond
hair. She's heavy, so much so that her arms don't hang
straight down.

"Don't know him," she says.

"That's Niles Cabro," says Cap. "I told you about him.
Remember?"

"Hmm," she says.

"Come on," says Cap with burlesqued gentleness.
"No one's going to hurt you."

She blushes. As though she's been complimented.

"Come on," says Cap. "I want you to meet someone."

She has an awkward flat-foot swagger, a hazy sense of
balance, a fear of her own weight. A wrist moves from
her swollen hip toward the wall, but Cap draws her to
the center of the room, to the clear place in front of me.
She wears pink pants and a white imitation leather
coat. There are ink marks, small drawings made with a
ballpoint pen, near her cuff.

"Hi," she says with a resonant deep voice, as though it were made on the bass string of a cello.

"Hello," I say.

One wrist taps against a hip. She looks to Cap.

"That's Niles," says Cap. "What are you supposed to say, remember?"

One of her eyes is dead, the other small: she sees a tiny world.

"Remember?" says Cap, taking one of her hands.

"Congratulations," she says.

Friends, along the walls, laugh, punch one another in the side, then look at her and moan, cartoon desire. One reaches out for her.

"I can't," she says. "I've got my . . ."

Five words is the limit. I want to ask if she can count to ten.

"She's lying," says Cap.

"Come here, sweetheart," says Lophead, his quickened hands playing the picnic table like a piano. "I want you to see something."

Stained envelope belches photographs onto the picnic table. Black-and-white sensuality. Suspicious of the floor, shuffling, she moves from the room.

"Look at this," says Lophead, picking one at random, holding it for her to see. "Jesus, look at that bush."

Giggling, crystal stung, he spreads the photographs on the table, arranges them as for a game of solitaire, then flips them in his lap, one at a time, and puts each in its appropriate pile.

"Spade," he says, pointing out a woman's pubic hair, then flips another. "Pretty well hung, huh?" He rubs her hand over the glossy surface. "Huh?"

She looks away: a courtly gesture. Her dead eye, touched with a cast, a spell, passes softly over me. I listen to her sluggish sigh, an idiot's wail.

"Can she count?" I ask Horse-T.

He laughs. "Sure," he says. "Oh, sure. Don't worry about that."

She leans her heavy thigh against Lophead's chair, puts her hands on his, stops him at one she likes. Her pride is dim, but strong: she picks carefully. Young girl straddles a man who sits in a chair, her back toward him, legs spread. Hairless slit, split bald fruit that reveals soft, irregular tissue.

"Yeah," says Lophead, "that's a nice one. I like that one, too."

A short red finger rubs a spot on the photograph.

"Hmm," she says.

"Look at that," says Lophead, flipping up another. "Jesus."

Friends whisper to one another, contest their cruelty, plan careful indignities. Lophead chuckles, gently fans her interest. She flips slowly through the pile, flattered.

"Yeah?" says Lophead.

She shrugs.

"Yeah?" says Lophead.

She looks shyly around the room, taps a wrist against her thigh, then whispers to Lophead.

"Niles first," says Lophead, "as an honor."

"What you want?" she says to Lophead.

He laughs. "Go on," he says, "go on and see Niles."

She looks around the room, not remembering.

"That's him over there."

The others turn away, polite, thinking I want her the way they do: alone.

"Aren't you going to watch?" I say angrily. "I would."

Horse-T looks at the turned back and shrugs.

"Aren't you?" I say to them.

"Easy, Niles," says Horse-T. "Let them be."

She takes off her plastic coat and spreads it on the

concrete before me. I try to see the drawings on the cuffs, the ballpoint hieroglyphics, but she's careful about turning the sleeves under. Awkwardly but quickly she kneels, relieved, more comfortable that way.

"What do you want?" she says with sluggish frankness. "A blow job?"

The limit: seven, learned by rote.

"Okay?" she says, leaning a hand on my leg, using the other to pull at coarse cloth. She struggles with her only ballast, an idiot's lethargy, tries to smile, shows greenish scum on white enamel. I help her with my clothes. Her small eye fills with pleasure, looks at what she wants. It's soft now, wrinkled, touched with a trace of grayish silt. She surprises me with an easy, graceful movement, as natural and practiced as a peasant woman filling her apron with delicate fruit: she leans forward slowly, lifts it with her fingers, takes it into her mouth, begins to suck. Her jacket squeaks beneath her knees. Her mouth is warm, faintly acidic. Shyly, slowly, Friends turn toward me, but it makes no difference. I don't want to hurt her. She rocks back and forth, in time to some private, oppressive tune, runs slippery lips over the end, stops, rubs it with her hand, always watching closely, curious about the way it stiffens. She takes a magician's pride. Her dead eye looks at the wall behind me, the other moves over split skin, the last of leaking blood, dark lumps and bruises, an oozing sore. She pushes her head under my hand, against it. She tries to swallow stiffened flesh, pushes it against the rough, open muscles of her throat, lets them contract slowly and gently against the tip. She rubs herself between her legs, opens her blouse and pushes broad, slopping breasts with adolescent ends against my knees. Plastic jacket squeaks against the concrete. At the first quick throb, she leans backward, pulling her blouse open.

"Come on me," she says.

It's like breathing. Molten pearl clings to her breasts, coalesces into shiny drops. With a filthy rag from the corner she wipes herself. Bruised ribs ache because I laugh so hard, so uncontrollably: she reaches with blunt, probing fingers for a sore.

"Hear that," says Lophead, with his back turned. "Must a been pretty good squirting."

Unfastening her pants, pulling them down, bunching them around her ankles, she falls heavily onto the concrete floor. But Cap doesn't give her time to finish. He rolls her over, takes her from behind. Lophead approaches, his penis in his hand.

"Fire me up, sweetheart," he says, kneeling next to her face.

Horse-T and I walk out, take Cap's car, drive until we find a bar that will serve us, a cocktail lounge with Frank Sinatra on the jukebox, a planetarium ceiling: bluish dome with pinpoint constellations.

"She enjoys it," says Horse-T. "I never touch her."

Horse-T gives me half of London's fifty dollars, and we spend it on good liquor.

"Dumb bastard," says Horse-T.

Little dipper. The North Star.

Horse-T slaps his thigh, orders another drink, although there's one sitting in front of him. His embarrassment, his struggle for a word reminds me of something.

"Touched," I say, because I really didn't have her.

"Yeah," says Horse-T. "That's the first time you touched a woman, ain't it?"

I nod. Horse-T chuckles quietly.

"What's that?" I say.

Horse-T and I sit in the bushes looking through the dusty leaves and thick branches into the yard across the street. Insects crawl around us.

"That," says Horse-T, "is a nineteen thirty-nine Indian."

High bars, goosenecks, and a tank that's shaped like a drop. It's bright yellow, and there's a black strip on the fenders. A twin, too.

"Eleven hundred cc's," says Horse-T.

It's got a leather seat, one that's cracked, its stuffing leaking out. And at the side of the tank there's a long lever for shifting, gnarled like a shillelagh. The clutch pedal is near the foot pegs, but it's only a narrow, greasy bar.

"You see that?" asks Horse-T.

"Death clutch," I say.

"Hmpf," says Horse-T.

"I want that Indian," I say.

"Sure you do," says Horse-T, "sure you do. That's why I brought you here."

Death clutch: it's accurate, precise. Just leave the Indian in gear at an intersection and you'll see. It doesn't take long. You hold the clutch in with the hard sole of your boot, and since the clutch pedal is just a greasy bar, your foot slips. And just like that you're under a truck. If you're stupid. Or lazy. You've got to put in the clutch with your right foot while you work the throttle with your right hand, but seeing as how the gearshift lever is on the right, too, you've got to reach over with your left hand to work that.

Horse-T opens his bottle of cold cheap wine, rustles in the leaves, gets comfortable.

"I've got to think," he says, "about getting that Indian."

I look through the bushes again at the house beyond the tree where the Indian is chained. It's a tall one, three stories, but it has a cancerous, jerry-made architecture. It looks like a junkyard of two- and three-room houses, one piled onto another. At the top, under the sharpest eaves, there's a stained-glass window, a round, gaudy porthole. The house is covered with yellowish clapboards, and there are vines from the flowerbeds along the front and sides clinging to them. The roofs, banisters, railings of the porches, and verandas are trimmed with obscene figures, a talented carpenter's enemies.

Horse-T sighs. I wait for a long time, watching the windows of the house, hoping someone will open one of the curtains. Finally Horse-T says, "It's chained up, isn't it?"

"You're right," I say.

"Fuck you," says Horse-T, looking up at the patches of sky between the leaves.

"That's some chain," I say, looking at links the size of fingers. "Let me have some of that vinegar."

I'm beginning to itch. There's something under these bushes, something that bites.

"Well, Niles," says Horse-T, "now you tell me how we're going to get that Indian. Seeing as how you're such a smart ass."

The grass in the yard is about two feet high, surrounded by a gap-tooth picket fence.

"Now my idea is," says Horse-T, "we just go in and take it. Anybody gets in our way and we just beat the shit out of them." He chuckles, swirls the wine around in its bottle.

"Maybe," I say. "Who owns it?"

"Don't know," says Horse-T. "Just saw it yesterday myself."

"Ain't rusted," I say. "Someone's been looking after it."

Horse-T grunts.

"And it's been there for a while." I point to the rough, healed scars in the bank of the tree.

Horse-T lights a cigarette and throws the match into the leaves in front of me. I put it out with my hand. We part the leaves again.

"Wish someone would come out of there," I say.

"No such luck," says Horse-T.

"Fuck it," I say. "Come on."

We stroll out of the bushes like we never been in them, like we never even seen a bush, and then walk easily across the tarred street. The ocean's down the hill about a quarter of a mile, and I can smell the salty air. Thump, thump, thump. I run Horse-T's bottle against the picket fence, trying to make as much noise as possible. Horse-T frowns, then walks to the gate and comes in with a gentlemanly air, as though he were an expected visitor. I hop over the fence.

"Look at that," says Horse-T. "The tires ain't flat."

The lock is rusted and about as big as a book. It looks like something from an old shipwreck. The chain runs through the spokes of the wheels and then around the tree.

"We could just take the wheels off and leave them here," says Horse-T.

"We ain't leaving without the wheels."

"It'd be easy," says Horse-T, "very easy."

On the second floor I see curtains drop together quickly, like a heart valve. The dumb bastard, I think, he's watching us.

I smile at Horse-T. "He'll be coming down soon," I say.

"Goddamn," says Horse-T. "Why did you beat that bottle on the fence?" But he swings his leg over the bike. Springs in the seat hiss, collapse into perfectly coiled snakes. He tries to look like Gunner Johnson.

"Berroooommm!" screams Horse-T, kicking the engine over. "Berroooommm!"

I throw my head back to drink the wine, squint in the sun, but I'm watching the house. He's already down to the first floor. I see more curtains drop together there.

"Berroooommm!"

Horse-T jerks the front wheel off the ground, stands on the foot pegs, leans into the turn, one boot just off the ground. I finger the lock, the scars on the bark of the tree. Horse-T squints in the wind, speed-shifts, flattens his body over the tank and handlebars. The grass is higher than my knees. It looks like I'm wading in a green pond. Curtains, at the window near the front door, swing together.

"Goddamn chain," says Horse-T. "Berroooommm, berroooommm!"

I'm looking dumb, wandering around the yard, drinking wine, chewing on a long piece of grass I've picked. And crazy, too. I dance a little with my arms out, hold a hello smile on my face. Ain't it a beautiful day! Horse-T drifts in the next corner, looking serious, tears quivering at the sides of his eyes in the wind. I'm thinking about dirt roads, just in springtime, when the ruts are deep, well defined, when they've hardened up. Then you ride that Indian over them, but you don't steer, you just let the ruts do it.

Gently and quietly a man opens the screen door and steps out onto the porch. He's heavy, but short, stunted, as though he has enough flesh for another half foot. Short, wiry legs, a heavy chest and arms. He wears a watchband that's twice the size of ordinary ones. Green khaki pants and shirt, a duckbill cap. He stands there on the porch, watching us, smiling. I know something when I see that smile.

"Berroooommm," says Horse-T.

"Hey!" says Duckbill, "Hey!"

"Berroooommm!"

"Hey!"

"What?" I say. "Can't hear."

"Hey," he says, moving closer to the railing, gesturing with one arm. "Beat it."

"Can't hear," I say, "the motorcycle's running."

"Berrooommerrrroooommm!"

"What's he saying?" I ask Horse-T.

"Can't hear," says Horse-T, "the motorcycle's running." But he knows it's time to stop. He makes a high-pitched whine, a steady flatulence through loose lips, a slow idling sound. He bounces up and down like a piston, then stops.

"Whew," says Horse-T, putting out his arm. "Vinegar."

Duckbill just looks at us. Sunshine! Trees! I smile. Duckbill makes a social gesture: he lights a cigarette and throws the match into the yard. Everyone's quiet so Horse-T laughs. Duckbill's got a vicious, stupid smile.

"What's that?" I ask. "You were saying something."

"Get the hell out of my yard!"

Horse-T groans.

"Oh," I say, "I see what you mean."

"What the hell," says Horse-T quietly. "A little Fred Astaire and then we take the bike."

I shake my head, hard enough for Duckbill to see. "We were just looking at your bike," I say. "What kind is it?"

He walks slowly down the steps, taking them one at a time, as though he were carrying a trunk on his shoulder. A heavy disease. One kidney, one lung, fused vertebrae, inflamed joints.

"None of your fucking business," he says.

Duckbill wears cowboy boots, but even with those high heels he only comes up to my chin.

"Sure," I say. "I can see that."

"Whew," says Horse-T, "something stinks."

He's right: it's Duckbill. Asylum odor, stench of worry and frustration.

Horse-T swings one leg over the bike, but I move around next to him. So I can do something to him if he moves. He looks at me like, Niles, you dumb motherfucker, don't be so sure I'm going to let you get away with this. You and your bullshit ideas.

We're all quiet: a still, silent choreography. Duckbill's arms are unnaturally large, limbs of the wheelchair or crutch. Horse-T sniffs like a prizefighter, rubs his thumb against his nose. A nasal huffing. The baseball cap keeps the sun out of Duckbill's squinting eyes.

"I like it," I say, pointing with showroom grace to the Indian.

"So what?" says Duckbill.

"Nothing," I say. "We was just walking down the street and we see this bike, that's all."

Shuffle like a duck, look like a fool. Ain't it grand to be alive! Smiles all around. Saliva bubbles on my lips.

"You seen it," says Duckbill. "Now get out."

"Does it run?" says Horse-T.

"Sure it does," says Duckbill. "Now get out."

"You want some wine?" I say, holding out the bottle.

Duckbill looks at me with death-ray eyes. Step a little closer, friend, I think, just step up and have a good look. That's right. That's it. The show's just starting, friend.

"Fell off a motorcycle," says Horse-T, pointing to me. "Had to scoop his brain back into his head."

Horse-T sighs.

I swagger like a cretin, show an idiot's genealogy, a history of mounting dogs, full-time masturbation. Duckbill's uncertain, confused, and that'll serve. He searches through his fifty years, finds in each the distillation of angry phrases.

I signal the bushes with my eyes. Horse-T understands.

"Get off that bike and get out of my yard," says Duckbill.

"Sure, sure," says Horse-T. "Sorry." When Horse-T smiles knives show.

I hop over the fence, Horse-T swaggers through the gate.

"And don't come back!"

It's so hot the street tar is soft. Its dusty skin splits

beneath our feet, reveals a viscera as black and shiny as licorice.

Duckbill stands in his yard, one hand on his hip, watching as we disappear into a bland camouflage, tarred pavement, houses quivering in the heat, abandoned automobiles.

"And don't come back," he says. "You hear me?"

The dumb bastard: he enjoyed it.

Horse-T and I walk down the hill behind the bushes, stepping over the trash. We sit on a discarded back seat and finish the wine.

"We need tools," I say.

"Sure we do," says Horse-T. He finds some burned-out tubes and breaks them, one at a time, against a radiator, then looks at me and starts laughing. "Sure we do."

Horse-T pleads with our car when I try to start it. It's some Ford. Horse-T holds his nose. "Roll down the window," he says with a comb-and-toilet-paper voice. He means it, too.

Car salesman tells us this is one fine station wagon, and he's right. Except for one thing. This Ford belonged to Farmer, and Farmer liked to go hunting a lot.

One problem, says Salesman, Farmer was a little lazy. What flashy clothes Salesman has.

Sometimes Farmer left dead deer in it and, regrettably, says Salesman, it smells. Put your head in there.

Whew, says Horse-T, with his eyes watering.

All you got to do, Salesman says, is drive with the windows down, and in California that's pretty easy because it ain't cold much.

"Little close in here," says Horse-T.

What we smell ain't deer, it's Farmer himself who died in this 1953 Ford station wagon. Heat doesn't make it much better either. One hundred and fifty-five bucks for this Ford and a dead farmer. Not a bad deal. He moans in the lining, makes the seat stinky, clings to the door handles.

Ford shivers, quakes, groans.

"Lazarus, honey," says Horse-T, "what's wrong, sweetheart?"

Gently, gently. Ford comes alive.

"That's it," says Horse-T with considerable pride.

We drive over canals, across arched Venetian bridges, over water that smells of sulfur, clogged with brown reeds, used tires, an automobile or two, covered with barnacles. I steer toward the warehouse that sits at the end of the street, a vagrant hump, isolated by lots filled with a bland and shiny moraine, tin cans, broken bottles, empty cartons, weeds. The warehouse has two doors, one inside another.

On the sidewalk a curious dog stops, sniffs, and begins to point at Ford, but Horse-T gives him a kick. The yelp echoes in the empty, hot street.

"Goddamn dogs," says Horse-T, pounding on the warehouse door.

"Open up," I scream, "we know you're in there."

"That'll get him," says Horse-T.

Lord opens the small door and peers slowly around it. Lord could be a midwife if women bled oil: his arms are stained to the elbow.

"Bang! Bang!" says Horse-T.

Lord puts the pistol into his hip pocket and says, "You shouldn't do that."

"Tools," says Horse-T, "tools."

He steps up and into the warehouse. The door is about a foot from the ground.

"How are you, Niles?" says Lord quietly, ignoring Horse-T.

"Tools," says Horse-T.

"All right," I say. "How about yourself?"

"Got one about ready," he says, pointing to a blue Cadillac.

The warehouse seems long and narrow except for the end, which is swollen with light, and there I can see jacks, tires, serpentine cables with caged bulbs at the end, rims, gaskets, pistons and engine blocks, a tool chest with its drawers drawn out like a pyramid's steps. Under the lights cars yawn. Horse-T finds a sack and begins to dig through tools on the bench.

"You want to drive it to Phoenix?" says Lord, pointing at the Cadillac again.

I'm thinking about that Indian, about Duckbill's smile. We're going to bring tools along, but we ain't going to use them.

"It's a safe one, Niles," says Lord, "just like off the showroom floor. Got papers and everything."

"This is it!" says Horse-T. He holds a large pair of clippers, a steel bird, a metal beak.

"Two hundred bucks, Niles," says Lord, "clear."

"Why, we just sneak up on the lock," says Horse-T, "snip! It's ours."

"Next week?" says Lord.

"Right," I say. "Next week, next month, next year. But not now."

"I wouldn't trust just anyone," says Lord quietly.

Lord's uncle lives in an old folks' home, but once he crashed out to spend a week with Lord. The old man didn't even get a chance to unpack: Lord had him driving a Chevrolet to Phoenix.

His mind's clear, says Lord, it's the body I should a thought about.

Lord's uncle comes back in tears, saying he loved every minute of it, saying he hadn't enjoyed himself so much in years. He's crying because he crapped on the seat.

"Take what you need and get out," says Lord.

"Berroooommm!" says Horse-T, holding the cutter like the handlebars of a motorcycle.

I fill the sailcloth bag with a ball-peen hammer, a cold chisel, wire, alligator clips, pliers. Horse-T rides the cutter around the warehouse.

"Bring those things back," says Lord, "you hear?"

"You ain't never going to see these things again," I say. "Fuck you."

Lord whispers over the open engine block. "I don't know what it is," he says, "but I don't want you bringing it around here. Got enough worries as is."

"Sure," I say.

"Don't want any lunatics around here," says Lord, glancing at the rifle on the wall. It looks like something out of a cartoon: the barrel is bent enough to shoot around corners. That's Lophead's rifle.

Listen, Niles, I own part of that warehouse, Lophead says, and if I don't it's time Lord got jacked up, anyway.

The rifle hangs now by one nail, like a horseshoe. Lophead says he spent the afternoon drinking wine with a towtruck driver. But he doesn't come here any more.

"Berroooommm!" says Horse-T as he steps through the small door.

Down the hill toward the ocean a kid chases a hubcap, hitting it with a stick. The sound punctures evening membrane, bluish light, tired air.

Horse-T and I eat cheeseburgers out of wax paper, wash them down with another bottle of Horse-T's wine. Farmer's so strong I can taste him.

"It's dark enough," says Horse-T.

* * *

We park the car and climb through the trash to the top of the hill where the bushes are.

"You're going to be disappointed," I say to Horse-T.

"The hell I am," says Horse-T angrily.

We crawl on our bellies beneath the branches into the hollow we left. Tools clink against one another in their sack.

"Keep those things quiet," says Horse-T.

Horse-T waits, breathes through his mouth. I make noise with the tools.

"Can't you keep those things quiet?" says Horse-T.

"He's smarter than you think," I say, chuckling because I've already looked through the bushes and seen something.

"How's that?" says Horse-T.

"Have a look," I say, pulling back a limb.

"Oh, no," says Horse-T quietly, "that ain't it at all."

The house is dark except for one light in a room near the top. There is no wind: the leaves are still as fossils, sharp stains against red stone, gaseous sky. The motorcycle is no longer in the yard.

"Someone beat us to it," says Horse-T.

I watch the lighted room. Membrane curtains, weak light. Too weak for reading. No one moves past the window.

"Goddamn it, Niles," says Horse-T, "we should have taken it this afternoon. Just kicked his ass and taken it."

"Shh," I say. "We got to wait."

"Shit," says Horse-T, taking a new bottle of wine from the sailcloth bag.

"He's still got it," I say. "He's just put it someplace."

"Where?" says Horse-T. "Where's he got it, smart ass?"

"I don't know," I say, "but he's got it."

Duckbill's counting on me to know that much. Which means he didn't believe us this afternoon: stories of sidewalk lobotomy, chucklehead insanity. I watch that window, wait, listen for cowboy boots on wooden floors. The wine doesn't do any good. Horse-T moans.

"Look here," I say, "now—"

"I'm not looking anywhere," says Horse-T. "That's probably the only thirty-nine Indian in this whole fucking country and you've fixed it up so we can't get it."

Horse-T scares people: he plays to the crowd, lets them think he'd do it, as a nervous tic maybe, like cracking a knuckle. There's something in his eyes, but it ain't for killing. I wonder if Duckbill's frightened.

"The light's on in that room," I say.

"So what?" says Horse-T.

"We got to think about that," I say. "Why do you suppose it's on?"

Horse-T has a drink that would cure a snakebite. "Bye-bye," he says. "I don't know you."

"We been watching for a long time," I say, "and I haven't seen anybody moving around in there. He ain't the kind of man who reads. Light's too dim for that anyway. He's the kind who moves around a lot. Don't think he could sit still for five minutes."

Horse-T ignores me, rolls over on his back, looks at the leaves, red sky.

"Now if he were asleep, the light would be off," I say, "but it ain't."

"Sure. Now that stands to reason, don't it?" says Horse-T. "Fuck you, Niles."

"So it looks like the light's on, and he ain't there. Right?"

Horse-T just looks at me.

"That means he ain't there but he wants us to think he is."

Horse-T rolls over and looks at the house, faintly interested.

"Now why," I say, "do you think he wants us to think
he's there, if that Indian is already gone?"

I find some pebbles and stroll toward the house.
There are street lamps, tall and streamlined, looking
like Martian periscopes, but they don't work. The pebbles strike the window with a glassy click, bounce and
rattle on short roofs. Empty rooms, oppressive space:
echo lingers, dissolves into a flat hum.

"He ain't there," I say.

"Well?" says Horse-T.

The grass is pretty tall, and that Indian's heavy. The
grass around the tree where the Indian was chained is
flattened down some, as though something had been
nesting there.

"All right, Niles," says Horse-T, "enough. Gumshoe,
sleuth bullshit. What's going on?"

It's dark, but I can see it, a narrow swath that runs
from the flattened grass to a swaybacked shed behind
and a little to one side of the house. Some of the shingles
are missing from the roof. It looks like a cob of corn
eaten by a man with only half his teeth.

"You see that?"

Horse-T nods.

"Looks like we're supposed to think he's upstairs and
the bike's in the shed."

I'm beginning to itch. Must be something under this
bush.

"Now that would be pretty easy," I say.

"But he ain't upstairs," says Horse-T, unaware that
he's begun to whisper again.

"He's in the shed," I say. "Any fool can see there ain't
a lock on the door."

"So we just wait until he comes out," says Horse-T.

"No," I say. "We got to go in there now."

"It's all the same to me," says Horse-T, "now or later."

The grass in front of the shed doors is flattened down, too, into patterns like those windshield wipers make. The street is hard now like cold wax. Somewhere, down near the water, a siren wails. Horse-T and I hop over the fence and begin to wade through the grass.

"I let that bike get away from me once," says Horse-T, "and I ain't letting it happen twice."

Nobody sits alone in a dark shed waiting for someone to come and steal something. Especially not Duckbill. He's got something with him.

"Why are you laughing?" says Horse-T, turning quickly.

"Nothing," I say.

"Well, if it's nothing, then shut up."

We walk right up the swath to the door, grass whipping our pants. I put a little spring in my step, let the sack swing back and forth, hum, "Fee, fi, fo, fum. . . ." Horse-T pulls the door, coarse and splintered wood, through the grass. I know Duckbill's around: calling card stench, as distinct as a fingerprint. The dark shed has a constricting atmosphere. Invisible objects push against rank air. Duckbill should get that on the market, I think, in an aerosol can. There's got to be a use for it. Dogs probably piss on his leg when he goes for a walk. Horse-T stumbles in the dark, hits something, rake, hoe, pail, makes it clatter on the concrete floor.

"Shit," says Horse-T.

"Where are you?" I say in a tone that's meant for Duckbill. "You got a light, don't you?"

The flashlight clicks on, but the beam is cut by the shotgun barrel that's beneath it. Horse-T tries to look menacing, but he stands with his foot in a bucket. In-

dian leans awkwardly against the wall, makes the
planks there bow. It's surrounded by a primitive spiked
defense of hoe handles, rakes, pickaxes. The shotgun
barrel is dark blue, streaked by light. Horse-T coils,
reaches for the handle of a pick. Above the light a red
button glows, the tip of Duckbill's cigarette. He blows
smoke over the barrel, makes it look as though the
shotgun has just been fired."

"I could have shot you both," says Duckbill, with the
red dot oscillating in time to the words. "That's within
my rights."

The light falls over Horse-T's hand, the pick handle.

"No," says Duckbill, but Horse-T doesn't move.

"You been waiting a long time," I say, drawing the
light toward me.

"It was worth it," says Duckbill, "wasn't it now?"

A sharp clatter in the dark: the light picks up Horse-T
kicking the bucket into a cluttered corner.

"Oh, Christ," says Horse-T. "I ain't going to do anything."

He takes a better grip on the pick handle.

"No," says Duckbill.

"I didn't want you to be disappointed," I say.

Outside the siren sounds like a landing spaceship.

"I'm going to disappoint your ass," says Duckbill, "in
about a minute."

Horse-T drags the pick handle a little closer to his
side.

"Tell him to stop it," says Duckbill.

"Ain't any need for shooting," I say.

"You'd be surprised," says Horse-T.

"Get out," says Duckbill.

"Okay," says Horse-T quietly, "all right."

"Get out!"

Duckbill's made intricate preparations: the flashlight's taped to the barrel.

The shed creaks at every joint, sways as though it's about to collapse when Horse-T slams the door. I pick a piece of grass and begin to chew on it, swagger through the yard like a hayseed outlaw. But Horse-T isn't having any: without even looking he walks through the gate and into the bushes across the street.

"That's right," says Duckbill, "you try it again. You come back, hear?"

I look around the yard, at the dark fluffs of trees against the sky, the single lighted window at the top of the house. He's got to use it, I think, he's got to. He's been sitting in that shed too long. I wait, smell the sea-tinted air.

"You hear?" screams Duckbill.

The flash of light inside the shed shows every crack, each missing shingle. The yard is filled with flying, splintered wood: the door explodes. The shotgun echoes in the empty street.

Horse-T waits at the bottom of the hill, sitting on a broken chair. I pick my way through the slowly flowing trash, around an icebox, a bathtub shooting junky rapids, chrome record racks, empty milk cartons, tires.

"Shit," says Horse-T when I get Ford started. "Let's get some gas and burn him and the fucking bike right out."

The gas station, a new one, has a large canopy that looks like an airplane wing, six islands, twelve pumps, a sign with bursts of red and blue flak that reads GAS WAR. In front of the garage and office there are cases of soft drinks, neat, bullionlike piles of Tahitian Treat and Canada Dry. And all around the canopy there's a welcome-home banner, GRAND OPENING.

I hear a drilling sound in the back of the station. The office and garage are made of some tinny alloy, and all the walls rumble. I find Cap behind the cases of oil, his head in a cleared shelf, a new drill in his hand. Corkscrew strips of metal spin at the end of the bit. It's Cap's first day on the job.

"It ain't got a peephole," says Cap. "Now what kind of station is that?"

Manager leaves at five. Cap has the place to himself until twelve, when he's supposed to close up.

"Shit," says Cap. "Well, I'm going to make a peephole."

Horse-T sits quietly on the cases of soft drinks.

"He's got to stew for a couple of days," I say, meaning Duckbill.

"Right," says Horse-T. "Fine. Just leave me out of it. Crazy people are more your line, Niles."

Horse-T has a school's-out expression.

I walk around the station, looking at the display models of hydrocarbons, the smooth, professional Tinker Toys. They're everywhere, on top of the pumps, hanging from wires, stacked in the office, sitting on cases of soft drinks.

"Hey," yells Cap over his stage-thunder drilling, "watch the pumps."

An automotive sheriff: Cap points the drill at a car that's just pulled up to one of the islands. It's a yellow Studebaker, a '51, with mud flaps and custom hubcaps. It's a convertible, too. The mud flaps have reflectors and the paint job looks like it was done in someone's front yard. The driver's got a brown three-dollar wig, but you can see gray around the sides of his head, in his natural hair. Powdered face, rouged cheeks, his cruising complexion.

I stand on the island and wring my hands.

"Ethyl," says Three-Dollar Wig.

"I pumped my last drop of ethyl," I say. "There's a gas war! Oh, where am I going to get more gas?"

"What about him?" says Three-Dollar Wig, pointing to Horse-T, who's filling Ford with gas.

"He's getting my last drop of regular!" I say. "You there," I yell at Horse-T, "stop that!"

"Huh?" says Horse-T.

"Oh, no," I say. "What am I going to do?"

"I'll come back tomorrow," says Three-Dollar Wig.

"Oh, would you," I say, "would you?"

"Sure," says Three-Dollar Wig.

"Thanks," I say, "thanks an awful lot."

Three-Dollar Wig bounces over the curb, honks the horn, grinds the gears, and finally pulls into the street.

"This place is right in the creep belt," I say to Cap, "ain't it?"

But he ignores me, intent on his drilling.

"It's got to be right beneath the toilet paper," says Cap, "otherwise they'll see."

The station is filled with new tools, buffed and shiny, as sterile as a surgeon's instruments, and sophisticated equipment, oscilloscopes and jacks run by compressed air. In a metal cabinet I find a uniform that fits. *Jim* is stitched onto the shirt. Talk about starch, I think. The cuffs and collar feel like smooth cardboard. Shiny strip down one leg. Some uniform.

The bit squeals, slips all the way through the wall.

"You got to keep the door locked," says Cap with a sly smile, holding the key to the women's bathroom, "so you can tell when they're in there. They've got to ask for it."

Cap sees me hanging the uniform on a new hook.

"You leaving at twelve?" I say.

He nods.

"But there's a gas war," I say. "The place should be open a little later."

"There ain't any gas war," says Cap. "That's just for suckers."

"Looks like a gas war," I say. "That uniform fit?"

Cap smiles and says, "Let me think about it."

Horse-T brings chicken dinners in cardboard boxes. We wash them down with warm Tahitian Treat.

"They take inventory once a week," says Cap, pointing to the racks of tires and batteries. "I got a few days."

Business is slow, but the bathroom's busy. It doesn't matter to Cap: young, old, fat, thin. He leans his head into the shelf, watches, not moving a muscle, holding his breath. He's got an eye like Long John Silver's.

"Whew," says Cap, "I'm going to miss that."

But he brings his car, the Mercury, around, and we load it with batteries, cases of oil, new tires wrapped with golden tape.

"You're in business," he says. "The manager comes at nine."

He takes the oscilloscope, too, puts it in the front seat: Lord's going to be a happy man.

"I got to see Lord," says Cap.

"Sure you do," I say.

Horse-T climbs into the Mercury, too, and says, "Enough. I'm going home."

Grand opening! I think, Come on in! But the station's empty. I watch with shopkeeper's anxiety the passing cars. The drunks roll in at midnight.

"Fill 'er up."

I pump gasoline. Hydrocarbons for the kids, coupons for the little woman. Cigarettes at cut-rate prices. Two packages for the woman who comes out of the bar across the street.

"My name's Ethyl," she says, "like the gasoline."

She's depression heavy, potato-fed, has a rotten tooth, greasy hair, one black eye. She has to navigate: walking isn't easy. A stained dress, shoes that almost match.

I offer her more cigarettes, but she refuses.

"I can only carry two," she says.

She looks behind the station, at the open ground there on which there's a few abandoned cars, their hoods open, engines gone, but otherwise in pretty good shape, the large wooden spools left by the power company, oil drums, lawn furniture without webbing, the stations overflowing trash bin. She looks at me, begins to speak, but then turns and walks back to the bar.

I pump gasoline: my pocket fills. A hundred dollars and some change. A drunk runs into the coffee machine, but I reassure him, fill his tank for nothing. I give him the last of the hydrocarbon models. The station has a pleasant odor. Coffee runs in the gutters of the islands.

"Look," says Ethyl, a half hour later, after walking across the street again, "lemme use that lot, huh?"

"Sure," I say.

"My name's Ethyl," she says, "like the . . ." But she stops giggling, squints at me, and says, "Oh."

In two hours she brings three of them from the bar, one shy and embarrassed, wearing glasses with large plastic rims, another with a scowl on his face, as though his dentures hurt. Honey, sweetheart, she says to them as they climb with her into the back seat of a castaway De Soto. The third, a thin and stunted man with quick movements and the drawn face of a baboon, who walks bent at the waist as though he were leaning into wind, spends a moment or two picking up papers in the lot to cover the De Soto's windows.

"You hold the money," she says to me. "I've got no place to put it."

"What's his pleasure?" I say, pointing to the third man, who walks now with a slow and careful gait, as though lingering sensation were a full tub of water.

"For six bucks," she says without smiling, "you can find out."

When the bar closes I have twenty-four dollars for her.

"Twenty-four rubles," she says with farmer's pride, as though she had grown them. She counts the greasy pile twice and is still convinced I cheated her.

"Beats me," she says, "how you did it. New way of folding bills or something."

"I didn't cheat you," I say. But she shakes her head and says, "You'll show me the trick sometime, huh?"

"Sure," I say.

She smiles, walks up the street to buy a chicken dinner and two bottles of wine, one of which she gives to me.

"Brrr-gun-dee," she says. "Straight to the head."

After her dinner I give her a uniform that has *Sam* stitched onto it and lead her to the bathroom, pulling in behind us the semicircular tub used for checking leaks in inner tubes.

"Make yourself at home," she says, taking off her dress and changing the water in the tub. "I ain't modest."

But both of us avoid her body, evidence of heavy years, sagging flesh that looks as though she were slowly melting. I sit on the closed toilet lid, explain about the peephole, tell her that every gas station has one. She asks if she can look sometime.

"I been in Europe," she says, momentarily awkward, smiling at some time-locked incident, some pleasant misunderstanding. She squats over the tub and cleans herself with quick, patted splashes, bidet-style. She washes her dress too, and hangs it on the aerial of the De Soto to dry.

"You've got to be out of there by nine," I say, pointing to the De Soto when she goes there to sleep. "The manager comes then."

"Fuck him," she says. "I'm sleeping till noon."

I pump gasoline, count my money, decide that a hundred fifty is enough for me: I ain't greedy.

The city wakes by color; dark sky, dark faces, garbage men sitting high in the cabs of their trucks; yellow sky, yellow faces, Orientals in their pickups, buying gas for the lawn mower; white faces appear at dawn.

"Gas war's starting," I say to a man dressed in white, his face and arms covered with flour. "Price is going down."

"What's it at now?" He asks.

"Half the price on the pump."

"Fill 'er up!"

Ping! Ping! Bells in the pump mark gallons.

"Gas war!" I say, startling a woman in a Plymouth station wagon. "We're going to run the competition clean out of business."

"Is it going down more?" she asks. "Maybe I should come back later."

I'm tired of making change: it slows business down.

"Don't leave!" I say. "I'll find out for you."

I run to the office, making a hurried phone call to the time operator: seven forty-five. Bad news for the competition.

"It's dropped to nothing," I say with wild eyes, my body trembling with disbelief. "Nothing at all."

"Fill 'er up!"

"Gas war!" I scream at a '53 Ford. "We're giving it away!"

"So what," says the driver. "Gimme a buck's worth and shut up."

But the word spreads: people ask to use the telephone, speak into the mouthpiece with tense, conspiratorial expressions. I run from car to car, setting each nozzle on automatic, finally get all of them working. The station fills. Every pump is chiming.

"Fill 'er up!"

Cars come and go quickly, as though from a pit stop. I give away the last of the tires and the batteries. The lines into the station grow: two lanes all the way down the block. There's a minor accident down the street and I see the drivers shouting at one another, pointing to a broken headlight, a creased door.

"How much longer is it going to last?" a driver asks.

"Until the competition folds," I say with a grim face.

But I watch the clock: eight-fifteen.

"Fill 'er up!"

I can't help it: I begin to laugh. Down the street at the Standard station someone climbs a ladder to the sign where prices are advertised. Petroleum! I think. The nation needs petroleum! Oil company executives, sitting in pajamas, wait for conference calls to go through.

Strategy? says one. We'll just run the lying bastards out of business. Agreements be damned. I always knew it would come to this.

I take the nozzle from a Dodge truck with a TV repair shop sign painted on its side, but the driver stops me. He has dyed, thinning hair, a black triangle that's combed straight back from his brow. A face so wrinkled it looks like an accordion. He peers into the opening of the gas tank, sees there's enough for a quart more, and says to me, "When I say fill 'er up, I mean fill 'er up, You son of a bitch."

"Sorry," I say.

On the other side of the station two women begin to fight over a nozzle. A man takes from the trunk of his Chevrolet a case of empty jars and begins to fill them. A child begins to scream. Soon most of the drivers are helping themselves, showing others how to work the pumps. A line forms at the telephone, too.

"Gas war," a man screams into the mouthpiece. "Free cigarettes and oil, too!"

Eight-thirty: I change in the bathroom, park Ford across the street and go into the bar. In the window there's a sign that reads: 8 A.M. TO 10 A.M. EYE OPENER, WINE, 15 CENTS.

Cap pulls up in front of the bar, sees Ford, and looks inside. He's driving a new Buick.

"I'm going to Phoenix," he says.

Where else? I think.

"You take care now," says Cap. And then he's gone.

The manager skids up in his Rambler, jumps onto the top of a pump, but no one will listen to him. A driver knocks him down. Manager has a smashed, bleeding mouth, a horrified expression: he stands on an island, not knowing what to do, listening to the pumps ring.

I walk across the street and say to him, "Turn off the power."

He's still stunned: large pupils, the color of oil.

"In the office," I say, giving him a gentle push. "The switch."

"Oh," he says.

I swear at Farmer, explain my anger, race Ford all the way to the beach, the shack.

"How's the gas war?" says Horse-T.

"Shh," I say, "quiet."

I hang my uniform on a hook.

"How's the gas war?" says Horse-T, laughing as he sees me count out half of the take.

"For the Indian you're not getting," I say, pushing the greasy pile toward him.

He frowns, but takes the money.

It's going to be a while, I think, arranging leaves, burrowing into the pile I make. I shake a branch, a rustling salutation to Duckbill, who passes up and down before membrane curtains, glancing every now and then toward me, at the clump of bushes. Indian's still in the shed. The door's been fixed with a new piece of plywood, and the chain hangs ceremoniously through two new brackets, its links clasped together with the ancient lock. Damp heat rises from the leaves; I pray for wind.

Days pass.

"Well?" says Horse-T, in the evening at the shack. "Well?"

I count the cigarettes Duckbill throws from the window. The yellow stains on his fingers are so distinct they look like birthmarks. At night he turns off the light, but I know he sits in his room, watching the bushes, thinking. Matches flare: I feel like a sniper. He has the sluggish, slowly changing habits of solitary men. Two cigarettes more the first day, three the second, an extra package at the end of the week. Membrane opens. Duckbill looks sadly at the shed. I shine my cheeks with leaves, hold them to my nostrils. The waiting's difficult.

Every morning, first thing, Duckbull checks the lock. My arms and legs are covered with small red bumps: I knew there was something under this bush. I watch a spider spin his web, dangle on threads of transparent glue, the thin strands I can hear squeaking from his body. His progeny fill with blood their membranous sacs, each one the color of ice, and carry them to slimy, squirming larvae. They treat me with supermarket respect.

"You want some wine!" I scream to Duckbill. "You want some wine!"

He sits on the porch, pretending he doesn't hear. He eats sullen meals, looks into his can like an aborigine into a large opened nut. Bread and fish, a little meat, tuna fish, sardines, and Spam. I count the cans he throws from the porch, stack my hours like soldiers in formation, one against the other, watch each day parade. Heat feeds upon itself, increases, makes the streets bleed black, viscous blood at the tires of each passing car.

I listen carefully: no TV, radio, phonograph, or ringing phone. Duckbill becomes embarrassed by the silence of his house, tries to avoid the few sounds he makes, the hollow banging of cowboy boots, the scraping of chairs across wooden floors, his mumblings. He takes a wrench from the shed and tries to fix a leaking faucet, but it does no good.

"It needs a washer," I scream.

Muttering to himself, he goes to the shed again, then stops, looks toward me, and throws the small pink ring into the yard. He makes an attempt at discipline, puts a piece of tape down the side of his bourbon bottle, and marks with a pen each hour's ration, but by evening the bottle's empty, and Duckbill spends an angry half hour looking through the grass for the washer. His heavy disease needs exercise: each morning he passes by the bushes, looks anxiously through the branches, sees my face, the expression of a Disneyland cannibal. He wanders around the yard, kicks like a child at the grass, fingers the new plywood door of the shed, the ancient lock, and takes the key from his pocket. Sweat falls slowly into the leaves, makes the slight, diminished sound of a drop of rain hitting a sail. That night, as a concession, I throw a pebble against the window of Duckbill's room, but he doesn't even bother to look.

"Well?" says Horse-T later, at the shack. "Well?"

I can still hear Farmer's laughter as we rode toward the beach.

"He's moved the bike back into the yard," I say, eating the cheeseburger out of wax paper.

Horse-T looks away from me, watches through the window the phosphorescent ocean, the waves' fluid skeleton against black water, beach, and sky. Lophead puts the spike in his arm, makes a small skin tent there, spends the evening gheezing, and says, chuckling, "Everybody's quiet."

"You're a fool," says Horse-T, striking once with his eyes. "It'll never happen."

I laugh, roll onto my cot, hearing the canvas cover crinkle like a snake's skin. It's hot under that bush: my brow is covered with body salt, each grain as sharp as ground glass.

It's true though. The bike sits under the tree again, chained there, leaning against it. And Duckbill seems to feel better for a while, too, thinking, as he sits on his porch, that he's tempting me. I've added bits and pieces to a leafy nest, beer cans and wax paper, empty cigarette packages, matchboxes, newspapers. White eyes measure me, consider a web between arm and body, head and shoulder. Insects devour fresh leaves, each as crisp as lettuce. I can hear them chewing, the swish of digestive juices. After a few days Duckbill realizes that I'm not tempted, but pleased: Indian's gravitating out of the yard. Every hour Duckbill checks the thermometer that hangs by a hook on the wall behind the porch. Heat and moisture grow. It's like sitting in a lion's mouth.

I tear the web, but the spider begins again, touched
by a blueprint nerve, trembling on a strand of shiny
monofilament. White eyes measure distance, serrated
leaves, a twig: all of his ancestors, since the last ice age,
would have built a web there. I charm him with quiet
whistling, listen to his pincers click. I count the days
backward and forward, try to divide the heat with
them.

Come on, I think, come on. I look at Duckbill sitting
on the porch. He no longer eats, has stopped changing
his clothes, lives on nicotine and alcohol alone. In the
morning he stops before the bushes, rubs his forehead,
then abruptly turns and walks back to the yard, where
he checks, once again, the lock that holds the chain
together.

In the evening, at the shack, Horse-T smokes slowly,
becoming as tired of the waiting as I am, and says,
"Well?"

"He wants to say something," I say. "I can see that."

"What's he going to say?" asks Horse-T.

I smile at him, go back to eating.

"Well?" I scream at Duckbill. "Well?"

But he doesn't speak.

Duckbill spends clocklike days, each one set by my
arrival. I catch him on his porch in a private charade,
the mime of some personal regret: an outstretched
arm, conciliatory smile, confessional gestures. I rustle a
branch, give him solitary applause, a shout of encour-
agement. He stops abruptly, ashamed and exposed,
then searches for camouflage gestures, makes a graceful turn to study the thermometer on the wall. Something bites: I slap the crumbling leaves. Nerves hum
with fatigue. Duckbill finally abandons all pretenses,

sits on the first step and stares at his boots, mouthing silent words.

I pray for wind.

At night he begins to eat again, opens can after can, gorges himself, finally gives up his greasy fork and grabs the fish and Spam with trembling fingers. He drinks a quart of bourbon, too, and later the empty house is resonant with his singing, *"Railroad Bill, oh, Railroad Bill . . ."* In the morning I see him wandering around the yard, illness for ballast, trying to walk off alcoholic insomnia.

"Hey," says Duckbill, standing in front of the bushes, looking for my face, "hey, it's for sale. Do you want to buy it?"

At the shack Horse-T chuckles.

"He's asking for more time," I say.

Lophead offers me his spike, his tie with sequins, but I shake my head. Horse-T chuckles, but he's frightened: he watches my trembling fingers, listens to disconnected talk.

"People never die right," I say to him. "There's always something."

"Right, right," says Horse-T.

Cigarette butts, like empty cartridges, lie on the steps around Duckbill's feet. When he looks up he smiles, as though he's thought of something. I begin to look for a good-size stone. The leaves beneath the bushes have been worn away, have crumbled into a rich and mulchy earth. Garbage, beer cans, sweat: these bushes are beginning to stink. Duckbill walks as quickly and lightly as he can to the Indian, fumbling all the while in his pockets for the key. The chain falls like a woman's robe. I look for a stone. Duckbill pulls the chain away from the bike and drags it through the tall grass. I look at the branch where I've marked the days:

fourteen. Duckbill drags the chain like a dead snake, lets the links, iron vertebrae, rattle on the steps. He smiles from the porch, eats a measured meal. I know he counts his years between each bite. I can only see Indian's seat, handlebars, and tank above the grass. Duckbill fondles the links of the chain, tries to wear them like brass knuckles. He's getting dangerous, too; at night I see him behind the curtains, holding the shotgun.

"Well?" says Horse-T.

"He's got more backbone than I thought," I say, "but he's cooking now."

"Sure," says Horse-T. "What's that?" He points to the stone I carry in my hand.

"Paperweight," I say, dropping it on the floor. But I take it with me in the morning.

The trash heap at the bottom of the hill is touched here and there with bright colors, soapboxes and Easter basket cellophane, festive liquor cartons, orange plastic that could serve sea and air rescue. I wait there in Ford for a few hours before slipping quietly into the bushes. Duckbill stands on the sidewalk with an anxious stare, suspicious as always of good luck.

"I'm still here," I say quietly.

"Where you been?" he says with tight, spiritless bravado. I cut another notch in the limb, then hold the stone in my sweating hand, let the moisture clean it. I examine the slight cracks, rills, the bits of glitter. Duckbill takes from the shed a roll of tape and begins to make a handle for his chain, wrapping one end of it slowly and carefully, pressing the sticky cloth into the center of the links. He works like a country whittler. The chain rattles on the steps as he turns it over, grips the handle, approves. His movements are self-conscious, definite, as though he labored in gelatinous air. Duckbill's careful about time, rolls the chain into a neat coil, leaves it on the porch, then takes the tape back to the shed.

"It's just sitting there," he says with a splintered voice. "It's not locked up."

I know he wants to part the leaves and limbs, but he can't bring himself to touch them. His clothes are body-weathered, eroded, without any shape of their own. He doesn't even take them off to sleep. He breathes through his mouth. And that stench, I think, he doesn't need to die. He's already for planting as is.

"It's just sitting there," he says. "You hear?"

Confusion plows his brow. His short legs and boots quiver in the three feet of hot air above the street's dusty, elephantine skin. He sits on the steps again, fingering the chain, counting its links.

"I hear you!"

The street, the cars near the ocean, the house, its verandas and porches, the motionless vines, trees and grass, the shed and Indian are fixed in stationary light. Crickets make a mechanical noise, like a rod turning in a worn bushing.

"I hear you!"

Duckbill swings the chain, makes the leaves explode, pulls at the branches. The chain wraps around a limb, and Duckbill goes after it, tripping over a root. He loses his cap, exposes his bald head, a semisphere of white skin above the tan line. I watch his boots kicking the dark mulch, his reaching fingers, the patches of white wood where the chain has torn the bark. He stands on the sidewalk again, making the iron links rattle against it. I know the bushes well, how to move easily through them. Duckbill pushes the branches aside, tries to find me, but the limbs snap backward, cut his face, head, and arms. He uses the chain against them, stumbles into the clump.

"That's right," I say, "give 'er hell!"

He tries to swing at the sound, hits his head against a large trunk, his shoulder against a thick limb. He falls, but still tries to roll toward me, wrapping the chain around his legs. It tightens when he tries to stand. I see a sanguine arm, blood running from his bald head, bits of froth.

"Over here."

He struggles with the chain, grunting, swearing, rolling in the trash, blowing blood out his nose, spitting. He frees himself, kicks at roots, tears leaves, falls.

"I hear you."

He sees me and stops, sits down on his haunches, realizing what he's done. He fingers his bald head, split lip, bleeding brow. His blood frightens him: he tries to move backward, away from stained fingers. His ribs convulse in heavy ripples as he tries to vomit. He strains, but it does no good: nothing comes up.

"Here," I say, handing him his cap and chain.

He sits on his haunches for a moment, breathing deeply, blinking, listening to the crickets, the ticking bushes.

"Take it," he says. "It's yours."

He slips to his haunches again.

"I don't need any help," he says when I move toward him, offering a hand.

He takes a branch with a trembling arm, pulls himself up, makes his way to the sidewalk.

"You'll come and see me sometime?" he asks.

Indian starts easily, idles without missing: Duckbill's taken good care of it. I look at the house, the blistering clapboards, carved railings, rotting shingles, Duckbill standing behind the curtains in his room. No, I think, dropping the stone into the tall grass, it's better to leave

it as is. He doesn't need a broken window. Death clutch
squeaks.

I pull up to the shack, riding proud as steel.

"Bye-bye," says Horse-T. "I don't even know you."

I prowl through the junkyard, finger twisted steel, hunt alloys, deal a hand of license plates. Mutant Cadillac sighs as I lift the hood. A deepfreeze still smells cold. A Buick has a broken steering wheel, a jagged point that pierced soft tripe. On the front seat there's a stain. Piles of automobiles sit like fat men around a fire. They eat out of rain-gutter trenchers, have spread around their haunches globs of red flesh, broken vises, bolts, fireplugs. A slow oxidation: rusty skins are formed and sloughed. Next to my foot there's a cotter pin, a toothpick. I try to emulate them, sit on my haunches, too, pick through the geared and unctuous carcass of a split engine block, become pleased when feasters accept me as one of their own. On the ground there are discarded objects, a catcher's mask without its padding, lobster-shell shin guards. I stop when I find the handle and chrome harness of a magnifying glass.

Safari ants bearing goods, bits of maggots, burn
where the sun finds itself again, focused by my glass.

Niles, Sis calls.

I watch the ants through the lens, make them grow to
the size of a thumbnail, see their shiny limbs quiver.
They've laughed in eyes, become drunk on vitreous
humor.

Sis is mine.

The bathroom door is closed, but not locked. Sis sits
inside.

Niles, Sis, says, crying, come in here.

She is not ashamed, sits with her legs apart, her hands
near a hairless slit.

I can't . . . she says. With a movement of her hand
she suggests running water. It is a perfect gesture.

It hurts where Uncle kissed me, Sis says.

I put the magnifying glass on the tile, wash my face.
Hawkeye knows, but does nothing.

He touched her with his mouth, I say to Hawkeye.

Hawkeye makes inventions in the basement, reads
electrical schematics from *Mechanix Illustrated*, tells
us his machines will make us rich.

You want a Schwinn, Niles, says Hawkeye, I'll get you
a Schwinn.

I shake my head.

Three years, says Hawkeye, speaking of Uncle, he
was in an asylum. But don't you ever let him know it.

I make Sis laugh, tell her stories of how, in about a
year, I'll put out Uncle's eyes, fill empty sockets with
salt, nail his skin to our garage door. But it happens so
quickly. He is an old man, our uncle, toothless, gum-
ming his food.

In a bathtub with lion's feet I find a sewing machine,
frayed fan belts, nails, piston rings, a glass ashtray that
looks like the remains of a Hiroshima window factory. I

walk around rusting metal, washing machines, a slaugh-
tered bus, think of a war cry, the scream of jets, Indians
howling at the airport, I search through open engines,
look for hints, clues, a residual patrimony.

My present from Lophead sits on the orange crate next to my cot. I hold it to the light, try to see what's inside: Lophead got a job, but most of us didn't believe him.

He comes through the door, mass-faced, in awe of corporate ceremony.

"I got a job," he says, digging for his works.

"Sure," says Horse-T, "and I'm Taj Mahal."

Lophead shrugs.

"I got a job," he says.

Horse-T takes five dollars out of his pocket and offers it to Lophead, but Lophead ignores it. He gathers his things together and begins to walk to the other room.

"Niles?" he asks.

"Good," I say. "I'm glad."

Lophead disappears through the blanket door.

Can you see? says Hiring Man, looking at Lophead's drifting eyes.

Can I see! says Lophead, running to the office window, reading the license plates of cars and buses a hundred yards away.

Can you sit? says Hiring Man.

Can you sit? asks Lophead with bewildered disbelief. What you think I been doing all my life?

Through the blanket we can hear Lophead playing "Buffalo Gal" on the harmonica. *"Won't you come out tonight, won't you come out tonight, and dance by the light of the moon. . . ."* Horse-T puts the five dollars on the picnic table.

Horse-T and I go outside and begin to pull the engine and transmission out of a new Chevrolet that someone left parked up the road last night. I set up a wooden A-frame and the chain pulley. Lord doesn't want the whole car, just the parts. Chain rattles in its metal block. We take a beating on the parts.

"He should pay more," says Horse-T.

"Lord's got distribution," I say.

"Sure," says Horse-T, "he needs it."

"What?" I ask. "The engine?"

"The five bucks!"

In the morning, before Lophead's first day, I see him at the kitchen sink. In a spoon he's cooking bits of cotton.

"Time for a little Ben Casey, Niles," he says. "Just a little cotton walk to get my eyes open. Today I gotta see."

The five dollars sits on the picnic table.

"Here," I say. I give him Ford's keys.

He cooks the cotton, stirs it with a toothpick, makes it give up its stale residue. Skin tent.

"That's better," he says.

He washes his face and rubs a crease into his pants.

"Good luck," I say.

He stops at the door.

"Listen, Niles," he says, "I'll bring you back a present. Okay?"

"Okay," I say.

It's cold and foggy in the yard. Ford shudders, but Lophead shows respect, gently chokes the engine. Ford leaves sluggish eddies in the fog. At the shoreline flat surf makes stones click. I think of presents.

Horse-T sits straight up in his bed, body quaking, too sleepy to move smoothly.

"He really went," says Horse-T. "I didn't believe him."

The five dollars still sits on the picnic table. Horse-T looks at it.

"Now why did he go and do that?"

"He wanted a job," I say.

"Shit," says Horse-T.

"Go back to sleep," I say.

"Right, right," says Horse-T. "You gave him the car keys, didn't you?"

I find breakfast in the icebox, half a cantaloupe and a frozen Mars bar. Chocolate goes good with melon. I put them on the picnic table, next to the five dollars.

"Didn't you?" asks Horse-T.

I continue chewing, put more food in my mouth, nod, smile at him.

"Don't hand me that," says Horse-T. "You're worried, too."

"So what?" I say.

Horse-T sits back in bed, leans against the wall like a Buddha, picks at the soles of his feet.

"Don't eat all the fucking food!"

I point at the five dollars.

"All right," says Horse-T, "enough. Leave me alone."

He pulls on a pair of pants, then sits opposite me at the picnic table. Friends drift in, each one saying, as he comes through the door, "Hear Lophead got a job." Around noon the fog is just a golden smear.

"Right, right," says Horse-T to the last Friend. "Come on, Niles, we got to finish that Chevrolet."

Chain rattles in its block. I clip sockets onto their handle and give them to Horse-T, who lies under the Chevrolet.

"He'll be back before two," says Horse-T.

Horse-T can't see me, but he knows I shake my head. "You're wrong, Niles," he says.

I get the last bolt, and Horse-T and I pull on the chain together as though we were hoisting a sail. The engine and transmission swing from the A-frame like a red, misshapen fish, bleeding oil.

More Friends drift in.

I drive Indian up to the store to use the telephone. It's a beach grocery: oiled flesh, the odor of suntan lotion, girls in bathing suits. Mothers whisper to their daughters, tell them not to look at me. Fathers look uneasy, gruffly grab their paper sacks of soft drinks from the counter. I smile at the daughters, buy cold wine, get change for the telephone.

"Hello," says Friend who owns a junkyard.

"Niles," I say. "Got a Chevrolet."

"Good," says Friend. "Nothing I like better than a Chevrolet."

"Bring a set of license plates," I say.

"Not so good," says Friend. "I'm doing you a favor."

"Sure," I say, "and I'm doing you one. It's yours for nothing."

"Good," says Friend. "Nothing I like better than a Chevrolet."

Horse-T sits at the picnic table, looking at the five-dollar bill. Friends sit around the room. About seven of them now.

"Well?" says Horse-T.

"He's doing us a favor."

"Not even twenty bucks?" says Horse-T. "Not even that?"

"No," I say.

Lord, who just buys parts, not the body, comes through the door. He looks at Friends sitting around the room and says, "I don't believe it."

"It's true," says Horse-T. "He got a job."

Lord sits at the table, shakes his head, takes a drink of wine. The five-dollar bill reminds him. Lord's all business: you should see him smile.

"I see you got something for me," he says.

He gestures toward the yard, the engine and transmission, unctuous trophy. Record catch: three hundred and fifty pounder snagged on Pacific Coast Highway.

"You don't pay much?" says Horse-T.

"Sure," says Lord, "but I got distribution."

"Shit," says Horse-T. "Don't I know it."

Lord counts fifty dollars out of his money clip and pushes it across the table to Horse-T. The money clip's got someone else's initials. Horse-T's eyes don't focus on the money, or on me when I take my part, but he puts his share into his shirt pocket. He leaves the five dollars on the picnic table. We listen as Lord backs his pickup under the A-frame.

"Distribution," says Horse-T.

Gulls land on the aluminum roof, and we can hear their feet scratching against it. Horse-T twists off the top of a wine bottle and tosses it at the ceiling.

"Goddamn birds," says Horse-T. "They go up there to crap. Wino birds."

Friends lean against the walls, sit on the floor. It's hot outside, but the shack still feels and smells a little bit like it did in the morning.

"We need a telephone," says Horse-T, twisting off another cap, "that's what we need. You and me, Niles, we're going to get one of Lord's cars, a good one with papers and everything, and we're going to drive it to Arizona. Then we'll get a telephone."

"Got one about ready," says Lord, coming through the door, "just like off the showroom floor."

"He wouldn't call," I say.

Lord sits down at the picnic table with us. He wears a brimless mechanic's hat.

"You been giving him money?" asks Friend.

"Get lost," says Horse-T.

Horse-T looks at the clock on the wall. It's two-thirty. Horse-T sends out for more wine.

"Did he say where he was working?" asks Lord.

"Niles?" asks Horse-T.

"Soda pop," I say. "Can you imagine him in a pop factory?"

"No," says Horse-T.

Birds' feet tap against the roof. The clock on the wall is a Coca-Cola clock.

"Well?" says Horse-T. "Doing what?"

"The bottles are washed out," I say, "and refilled, but sometimes the washers don't get everything out. So there's this conveyor belt that carries a line of filled bottles past a light so you can see if anything's inside. He's supposed to sit on a stool and watch the bottles go by."

Horse-T shakes his head.

"It ain't true," he says.

"Hiring Man told him," I say, "people put crazy things into pop bottles."

"What can you put in a pop bottle?" asks Horse-T.

"I don't know," I say.

Gravel rattles on the road, but it's only Friend who

owns the junkyard. He's driving his towtruck, a new one with a long aerial and a bank of lights on the roof. There are halves of tires over the front and rear bumpers so that the truck looks like a tugboat. The radio's on loud, and I can hear the hello-central voice of the woman police dispatcher.

"Wish he'd turn that down," says Horse-T.

I do, too: Hello Central makes me nervous.

"He better not come in here," I say, "without some money."

But Junkyard Friend understands. He just changes license plates, hitches up to the Chevrolet, and begins to tow it out of the yard, like an Indian litter behind a horse. He stops in front of the window.

"That's a lot of Chevrolet for nothing," says Lord.

I nod.

Junkyard Friend sits in the cab of his truck, waiting, looking in the window, Hello Central speaks of codes.

"He's got a good Chevrolet with no engine," says Lord. "If he's smart . . ."

"He's smart," I say.

"Well, then he just waits for a smashed-up Chevrolet with a good engine. That way he makes about fifteen hundred."

"Plus getting paid for towing," I say.

"Sure," says Horse-T.

Junkyard Friend waits in the cab of his truck.

"He's afraid to ask," I say.

"He should be," says Lord.

That's some truck, I think; got chrome smokestacks behind the cab, and spinner hubcaps, too.

"That radio is driving me nuts," says Horse-T.

Junkyard Friend wears a heavy ring, and he taps it against the steering wheel.

"Tell him, Niles," says Horse-T. "But next time he ain't getting a Chevrolet for nothing."

Junkyard Friend watches me as I come to the window.

"He got a job," I yell into the yard. "He ain't been back since this morning."

Fifteen hundred, I think. Junkyard Friend knows better than to hang around. Wisps of smoky dust rise from the ruts in our road as he drives out. We can hear Hello Central all the way up to the highway.

"Good," says Horse-T. "I was getting tired of looking at that Chevrolet."

The roof ticks with heat. The gulls can't stand it so they fly down to the beach, peck in the sand, dodge incoming waves.

"People pay you to do funny things," says Lord.

Horse-T laughs.

"What's so funny?" Lord asks.

"Niles?" says Horse-T.

Hiring Man says to me, Can you drive?

Can I drive? I say. I cut my teeth on the freeway.

Can you pick things up? says Hiring Man.

Sure, I say, I can do that.

You got a job, says Hiring Man.

Hiring Man gives me white clothes like a doctor's and the keys to a new white panel truck. Truck's got a seal on both doors: Coroner's Office. I sit in a room with other men, each dressed like me. Everyone watches the phone. Ring, you bastard, they think, come on and ring! No one moves: the starched rustling is too much. I creak over to the coffee machine. A noisy potato man. I dream of a hundred dollars, the week's prize, calculate my earnings to the second. The other men stare at my noisy sleeve when I sip the coffee. Their eyes avoid my novice's shoes: suede wing tips. Ring, you bastard, I think. Telephone rings. It's yours, one of them says, handing me an address written in an electrocardiogram script. On Figueroa, he says. Ah! Figueroa, my favorite street. Alky, he says, you should have an alky. Alkies never weigh much, he says. I hunt addresses, look for death houses, find a clean hotel with a cop waiting in the lobby. Starched pants and sleeves creak down the hall. In here, says Cop. Thank you, I say. There are empties everywhere, under the mattress, in the bathroom, in the pockets of the coats that hang in the closet. On the bed I can see the legs and buttocks of a woman. Her head and torso are between the bed and the wall, so she's bent like an L. Sticky fluid on the floor beneath her lips. Been that way for a couple of days, says Cop, sniffing the air. Colleague was right: she's as light as a manikin. What you going to do about that? says Cop, pointing to the stretcher where she sits, still bent like an L. I don't know, I say. If you push her back, says Cop, her legs'll come up. That's right, I say. I hold her legs down and push her shoulders, but she creaks at the waist, as though she were going to break in half. Cop sighs. Oh, no, lady, I think, don't break in half. She rides behind me in the truck, sitting up on the stretcher, covered with a starched sheet, a small white tent. I avoid the rear-view mirror and think, I know what I'm going to do. I'm going to steal this truck.

"Sure," I say to Horse-T.

"You should have stolen that truck, Niles," says Horse-T.

"I would have had it," I say, "but I had to drop her off."

"No," says Lord with a certain amount of pride, "you shouldn't have taken it. I only deal in luxuries."

Lophead stands in the door. He carries a small paper sack.

"What's going on?" he says, looking around the room.

"Nothing," says Horse-T.

Lophead puts Ford's keys on the table and picks up the five-dollar bill.

"How was it?" asks a Friend.

Lophead folds the five-dollar bill and puts it in his pocket. "Why all the people?" he asks.

"They're just leaving," says Horse-T.

Friends know he means it. They leave through the door and windows.

Lophead puts the bag on the picnic table. "That's a present for you, Niles," he says. "I thought you'd like it."

Lophead finds his works on the sink and takes them into the other room. The bag sits on the table.

"Aren't you going to look at the present?" says Lophead through the blanket door.

Brown paper rattles. I know Lophead's listening.

"Hold it up to the light," he says.

He waits until he hears me put it back on the table.

"Thought you'd like it, Niles."

"Christ," says Horse-T.

"People put crazy things into pop bottles," I say.

"If it hadn't been for that," says Lophead, sticking his head and arm through the door, "I wouldn't have lasted until noon."

Horse-T laughs.

We climb into Ford, take Lophead out for Mexican food. Farmer's been sitting in the sun all day and he's rank. In the restaurant sullen braceros revolve around the jukebox, each carrying a tall, thin bottle of beer. We watch the Mexican woman behind the counter preparing the food, stepping over the frying pans she keeps on the floor. Nothing Lophead likes more than Mexican food.

That purple color could have leaked from any neon tube. I sit on my cot, holding the bottle to the light, looking at what's inside: the tampon. I have the bottle that touched her lips, a private article, her fertile blood mixed with carbonated grape.

H

orse-T eyes an all-night gas station, takes from the icebox the pistol he keeps there in a Wonder Bread wrapper.

"That ain't it," I say.

"Well, Niles," says Horse-T, turning quickly from the icebox, holding the pistol in his hand, "you tell me what is."

I've got fifty dollars taped to a cot leg. Horse-T and Lophead get half.

"It ain't money we're running out of," says Horse-T, "so much as ways to get it."

You can't live by midnight auto, not at Lord's prices. Most hype is good only once.

"Let me think about it," I say.

"You do that, Niles," says Horse-T, "and when you're done we'll think about that gas station."

My desperation shows:

I wake quickly in the morning, aware that someone's watching me. My body's curled, blanket's pulled to

nose. The fog is cold. A young woman sits on a chair at
the head of the cot. Dark hair, blue eyes, skin with a
deep and rich coloring. Her belly's swollen with a nine-
month growth, engendered tumor, kicking child.

"I'm from Phoenix," she says.

"I never been to Phoenix," I say.

I listen, not saying a word, while she explains. She
describes a man who has reddish hair, a birthmark the
color of cranberry juice on his forehead and cheek, and
insanity's broken expression. One of Lord's drivers, an
escapee, but I never asked from where.

"He's not the father," she says.

"Good," I say. "That'll make one less idiot around."

"He said I could stay here," she says.

I drive Ford down the gravel road about a hundred
yards and park it next to the grove of eucalyptus where
there's shade, then bring from the shack things she'll
need: pillows, blankets, a roll of toilet paper, books, a
transistor radio, two galvanized tubs, a sheet to cover
the windows, a piece of canvas to make a tent off Ford's
rear door, and a chair to put under it. I explain that the
toilet facilities aren't the best, but if she needs them,
they're right out in the middle of the grove. I tell her at
night I'll bring canned food and water for bathing.

"It stinks in here," she says.

"Keep the windows rolled down," I say. "You'll get
used to it."

She follows her belly to the shack to get a Thermos
filled with water and ice. Horse-T comes through the
blanket door, looks out the window at Ford grafted into
the landscape by the tent, looks at the girl, her belly,
and says, "What's going on?"

"She needs a week," I say, "maybe less."

"Here?"

"Right," I say.

"What if she dies," says Lophead, sticking his head through the blanket.

The girl studies her shoes, new ones, panic's luxury, shiny red leather, hand-tooled designs.

"Just what we need," says Horse-T, "cops sniffing around here, asking about a stiff."

"I'm not going to die," says the girl.

She walks through the door, along the gravel road, picking her way carefully, as though she were walking on the slippery stones of a stream.

"Christ," says Horse-T, looking at the Coca-Cola clock, "I been awake for ten minutes and I'm already pissed off."

"No need to talk about dying," I say.

"Shit," says Horse-T as he sits at the picnic table and puts his finger in the mouth of a wine bottle. He doesn't want to smell last night's dregs.

"I'll tell you what," I say. "If she dies, I'll drive that Ford to San Diego, take the plates and registration, and leave it there."

"Then we lose a Ford," says Horse-T.

I begin to laugh.

"See," says Horse-T, "you're getting shaky. And this ain't the time for it."

Lophead shows his worried face at the blanket door.

At night I bring her water for bathing, a new Coleman, Horse-T's pistol in its Wonder Bread wrapper.

"Funny people come around the shack," I say.

Wrapper's weight gives its contents away. She doesn't bother to look inside.

"I seen funny people," she says without smiling.

She's spent the day in the sun, and she's still wearing her bathing suit. Her belly looks like a brown, rising loaf. Coleman breathes, coughs through vaporous membrane, then hisses, burns sharply.

"My name's Cathy," she says. "Cathy Hobart."

I shake my head and say, "You don't want to use that."

She laughs.

"What do you suggest?"

"Something ugly," I say. "Look in a phone book."

I explain about names, show her my list of them. The first five have been scratched off, the best of the lot, but the others would serve if I had a place to use them. I explain about one-time hype. You get a social security card in a phony name, and a job at the stadium selling hot dogs. That stadium looks like a cement crater. Before the third quarter, before Hiring Man collects, you hide the Coca-Cola hat and aluminum hot dog box and leave. One time only: $150.

"You can make short change, too," I say, "when something happens on the field."

She studies her shoes, looks at Coleman, nods.

I explain about radio games, those in which you guess the scores of Saturday's games, and how you go about winning: run an unsealed envelope through a postage meter on Tuesday, flip on the radio Saturday night, copy down the scores, drop the envelope into the mail. Earliest postmark wins. Radio station's letter comes to Lord, and he says, dropping it into my hand, "Don't ever use my address again." Inside there's a check for a hundred dollars and a note from Publicity Man. "I can't prove anything, but if you want to play again, don't use metered mail."

"That's what you do?" she says.

I stop laughing.

"Yeah."

Brown, swollen belly. I think of proud, Old Testament names.

"You'll need a good one," I say, "a good name."

"After this," she says, "I'm only going to use my own."

I start walking back to the shack.

"Hey, wait a minute," she says.

"I was talking about the kid," I say.

She stares at me for a moment and says, "You don't have to go."

I shake my head.

"You want to feel him kick?"

In the shack Horse-T's about to speak but my face stops him. He goes back to staring at the few bills and coins, the last of the money, spread on the picnic table.

"There's not even enough to count," says Lophead.

In the morning I say, "Okay. I'll go to Phoenix."

"Risky," says Horse-T. "You don't look like the kind who should be driving a new Cadillac around."

"Sure," I say, "and you're getting ready to shoot someone's ass off for fifty bucks."

"I wasn't going to shoot anyone," says Horse-T.

Lord's all smiles when I tell him what I want. It's simplicity that pleases him: he needed a driver so he just paid less for parts, knowing I'd come around sooner or later.

Cadillac's the color of meat.

"Good driver's hard to find," says Lord.

"That's right," I say. "Maybe parts'll be a little more expensive the next time you come around."

Lord laughs and says, "Maybe I'm not buying parts from you any more."

I glance at a crowbar on the floor.

"You can always drive," says Lord. "It's better than some silly shit like jacking up a gas station."

He hands me the papers and the keys. Cadillac's got tinted glass, an FM radio, seats covered with fragrant leather.

"Consider it a promotion," says Lord.

I pass El Centro, the flat, reeking fields around it, neat squares redolent of fertilizer, onions, and rich earth, and the workers in them, still, bent, trapped on a row. Water jumps like a silver fish from a rusted pipe. There's farm machinery, too, all exposed gears, rods and blades, black mufflers and rusted tin hoods. When I come to the canals I'm tempted to stop and swim, but I continue, passing dunes and the tar-and-wood stage road that runs through them, watching, at sunset, the desert's scrubby skyline, stopping only once for gas and food at a milestone luncheonette and service station, always keeping an eye on the rear-view mirror, waiting for a small-town cop, a commander of a South American regiment, dressed in jodhpurs, gold braid and epaulets, knee-high boots and Sam Brown belt to match, driving a car with fishing-pole aerials, its roof crowned with amber and red lights, silver, drop-shaped sirens. That's a mighty nice car, boy. Where'd you get that car? That Cadillac? Stretched neon scar in the desert sky: Phoenix. I drop Cadillac off, collect two hundred dollars, and catch the Greyhound home. A soldier mumbles songs and slits, with a switchblade knife, a souvenir of Mexico, all the empty seats.

I put seventy-five dollars on the picnic table, roll onto my cot, and say to Horse-T, "Lord's smarter than I thought."

"Sure he is," says Horse-T.

I turn toward the wall.

"No more parts. Is that it?"

"He said we could drive," I say.

"Shit," says Horse-T, opening the icebox door. "I got an appointment at a gas station."

He rummages around on the bottom shelf, looking for the heavy Wonder Bread wrapper.

"And then I'm going to see Lord."

The cold paper makes a sharp, irritating rattle.

"It's not there," I say. "I gave it to her. Out in the Ford."

"It was mine," says Horse-T angrily. "That was my property."

He slams the door so hard the Coca-Cola clock falls from the wall with a plastic clatter.

"Goddamned clock," says Horse-T, looking at it as though it were a snake, some threatening beast or element. "Man's got an appointment and he can't even get his property to keep it."

He sits at the table and drinks scarlet wine from its green bottle.

"I'm thinking about something for Lord," I say.

"Ain't necessary," says Horse-T. "Me and my property already figured it out."

Horse-T mumbles something else, but I don't hear it: sleep comes like someone slamming a door.

"How are things?" I say, in the morning, standing under Ford's tent. The air is hot. She sits in her bathing suit, watching the fishing birds, spume and flash of breaking waves.

"I'm sorry about the name," she says.

I shrug and reach out for her belly, the moist and warm skin, and feel a shifting, indistinct shape.

"It's waiting for a full moon," I say. "High tide. Something like that."

But my face gives away what I'm thinking, something Hawkeye told me: Niles, there's only one rule in science, and that's if it can happen it will happen.

"Sure," she says.

I kill the day in the shack, spend the hours with tedious undertakings, looking through stale newspapers, the business opportunities in them: I consider purchasing, for ten thousand, cash, the world rights to a patented device, a piece of metal shaped like an I that has suction cups on one side and a belt on the other, a machine for strapping a dog in the tub when you want to give him a bath. There are survival manuals in the shack, and I look through them, thinking of making snow houses, desert stills, taking note of the fact that all mosses and lichens north of the Arctic Circle are edible.

In the evening Lophead returns with a sack of Chinese puzzles.

"Look at that," he says, holding up a globe of carved interlocking pieces. It looks like a model of a world where all countries are shaped like squares or rectangles.

Lophead gives me the instruction sheet, takes the puzzle apart, and begins to put it together.

"Fucking puzzle," he says.

Hours pass, but he stays with it, thinking the puzzle contains some mystery, some usable tool: he feels the same confusion working it that he does each morning.

A horn honks.

"Shit," says Lophead. "Let me see the answer."

I hear the horn again, and then I'm out the door, running.

She lies in Ford, knees drawn up, sweating, frightened.

"Two pieces of string," she says, "and a pair of scissors."

I try to take her hand, but she shakes her head and says, "Don't touch me."

"Okay."

I leave the scissors and string next to her side and then sit on a chair in the fog and listen to her grunting, screaming, swearing like a sailor.

Horse-T comes down the gravel road, but he doesn't

see me because of the fog. I hear him say to Lophead,
"What are you working that shit for?"

The horn blows again, later, much later when the fog
has begun to lighten. I find her in the front seat, tired,
not even trying to smile, holding in her arms something
wrapped in a clean sweatshirt. I see a ball of stained
cloth, the scissors smeared with blood. She gives me the
child and I move him from hand to hand.

"I don't know," I say.

The sand squeaks beneath my boots.

"Hey," she screams, "you son of a bitch."

With the child tucked into my coat I drive Indian
over damp streets, the water on them stained blue by
morning light. The produce section is filled with
wooden stalls, piles of rotting garbage, silent, busy men
unloading trucks: it's too early to speak. But I find what
I want in one of the abandoned stalls: the child squirms,
screams, protests the cold metal of the curved scoop.

"Seven and a half pounds," I say, pushing the child
back into Ford, into her arms. She takes a careful inventory, counts fingers and toes, looks into crevices, under
arms, makes sure no damage has been done, then rolls
up the window.

When I wake, she's gone. The tent's down, folded,
and placed next to the neat pile of other things, tubs,
the flashlight and Coleman, blankets, transistor, Horse-
T's pistol. The back of Ford has been scrubbed clean
with sand.

"Cat got your tongue?" asks Horse-T from the door.

I become interested in facts.

"Cat got your tongue?"

Days pass. I try not to move.

"You stink, Niles," says Horse-T.

From a box I rip a piece of cardboard, and with a grease pencil I write across the top, *Niles' facts.*

I look everywhere: in old almanacs, in the gossip columns of the newspapers, in conversations overheard on trains and buses. I remember holding a stethoscope to the wall. Thoughts surface like brown trout after flies.

"As a machine the human body is thirty-three percent efficient."

Horse-T watches from the door.

I sit on my cot, a blanket draped over my shoulders like an Indian's. Around my feet are the trappings of those who lived here: tabloid newspapers, mismatched boots, motorcycle parts (a sprocket, some chains, handlebars, rings, pistons, gaskets), wine bottles with candles stuck into their necks, their bases covered with gaudy wax stalagmites; rags, a T-shirt from Pacific Ocean Park, a torn jacket, a heavy Mexican blanket, a wooden box filled with tuning forks. Along the wall are castaway possessions, adrift in cardboard boxes. Lophead keeps them neat, waiting for their owners' return. Through the window I see the sea scarred with kelp, and the fishing birds, hovering over the water, then diving. Something flashes in a beak. Rag curtains form a face, a severe chess piece.

I make excuses years out of phase.

Sis had a hairless slit. Uncle touched her there with his mouth.

Hawkeye drives his green Chevrolet through the park, beside the bridle paths, the dark horses cantering on them. Burned sits in the front seat on the right-hand side next to the door, her fingers playing the same tune over and over again on the chrome handle. Sis and I sit in the back seat.

He was drunk, says Auntie in her house, the house we flee from now. He was drunk and he didn't mean anything.

Hawkeye finds me in the kitchen, looking at the rack of newly sharpened knives, hanging like icicles from their hooks, bright and shiny, the color of Auntie's vicious, practical tears.

Come on, says Hawkeye, we're leaving.

We drive through the park, past the bridle path, the dark cantering horses, and Burned says, Well, why didn't you do anything?

He was drunk, says Hawkeye angrily, aware that Burned watches the speedometer, that she's waiting for it to climb. Hawkeye knows she'd wait for sixty anyway.

Why didn't you do anything?

Hawkeye pushes the pedal, but keeps the needle just shy of crucial speed.

Sis doesn't want to hear a word: she squeezes my hand, looks at the horses, the sun on their black, shiny coats as they pass through the splashes of light that filter through the trees.

Burned thinks of a hard, sliding bounce, grated asphalt devouring flesh. The front door, on the right side, opens just a crack, and I feel wind rush into the back seat.

Well, says Burned, why didn't you?

Hawkeye toys with the needle and says, You want me to smack you?

And that's all: with a shrug, constantly moving her eyebrows up and down, Burned closes the door.

I want a horse, Sis says quietly to me.

But I think she wants to feel a strong animal between her legs.

Sis lights incense before her shrine, that nightstand on which there are flowers, hammered brass, doilies, a small portrait of Krishna.

She tried to commit suicide, didn't she, Niles? asks Sis.

But I know now that Burned opened the door because she wanted pity for herself alone, being desperate enough to steal any grievance.

Hari, hari, hari . . . chants Sis.

In the morning, after the fit, Burned sings, *"Ka-ka-ka-katie, you're the only ga-ga-girl for me. . . ."*

I look for facts:

"Most suicides occur on Monday morning, between nine and twelve."

Horse-T looks over my shoulder and says, "Right, right. How about next Monday? That suit you?"

I pull the blanket around my shoulder, nod, laugh like a drunken chief.

"Right?" says Horse-T. "Right?"

Lophead brings catalogues of this year's new cars.

I eat cheeseburgers out of wax paper, wander through a store which only sells clothes made by machines gone amok: pants with three legs, zippers sewn into knees, gloves with six fingers. I see a woman digging through the piles of mutant clothes, worrying over the perfect fit. I tell her I'm sorry.

"You are seven times more likely to die during the twelve months after the death of someone you cared for."

Niles, says Burned, Niles.

I stand in the hall outside the bathroom. I carry a magnifying glass, a killer of safari ants.

Your father says I'm hairy, she says, so I shaved.

She wobbles on high-heel shoes, wears a terry cloth robe.

You want to see?

I shake my head.

Here, she says, look.

I shake my head.

She pulls the robe open: bald, two-fingered hand.

Bluish stubble, like a man with a heavy beard. She laughs, then becomes ashamed, accuses Hawkeye.

Before we go in there, she says to him, you tell Niles.

Every Sunday afternoon, just like clockwork, I think, they get clean and drunk enough to touch each other.

A whiff of steam from the bathroom, four soap-caressed legs.

Before we go in there, she says, you tell him. You tell him you love him.

Hawkeye's unsure hand.

Yes, he says, yes.

Clipped ass recedes.

He's not the kind, says Burned, you understand.

I nod, reach for the magnifying glass. I'm a ticket-taker for Sunday afternoon.

Coca-Cola clock marks time.

I walk around the room, open boxes, examine possessions, clothes, old letters. A lazy interest. I'm surprised to find myself going through my own: a red cowboy shirt, white mother-of-pearl buttons, four of them on each cuff.

Rodeorider stands in dusty sunlight, surrounded by pickup trucks and horse trailers. Around the arena are stands filled with people. On a platform musicians play country music. Talk about style, I think: bright green shirts, tailored pants, guitars ornamented with mother-of-pearl. Sea-song cowboys.

You listen good, says Rodeorider, you hear me, Niles?

Behind us, next to the chutes, men with broken teeth drink bourbon out of pint bottles.

I may ride a bull every now and then when I'm drunk and crazy enough, and I know something about staying on. You hear me?

I hear you, I say. I wish I had a pint bottle.

Sis stands next to Rodeorider. She smiles at me, then turns toward the musicians. She smiles, but she's worried.

I'm going to ride one of those bastards, I say.

Sure you are, says Rodeorider, I already put up your fee. I'm pleased with Rodeorider's hard professionalism.

When you sit down, he says, you wrap the rope around your hand until it hurts. You hear me? It's got to be tight.

I nod.

Then you move your balls to one side and you sit on

your fist. Ain't nothing keeping you on except for your glove and the rope. Hold your hat in your left hand and spur with both legs. That gives you balance.

Rodeorider's got style, I think. Jesus, could he spur. You spur with both legs, he says.

I laugh, drop the shirt into the box, begin to go through my other things: a shiny suit, a couple of shirts, mismatched pairs of socks, stained underwear.

Jesus, could he spur.

"I just wanted to be a good survivor," I scream at Horse-T, "that's all."

He laughs and says, "Don't look like you made it."

Stinking ward, moaning bodies encased in white shells. Hawkeye's mother's dying. Broken bladder, something vital ruptured: her leg fills up with piss, swells, looks as though it alone were pregnant. I stand before the bed, expecting subtleties, laser beams and magic, but I'm wrong, then surprised by primitive treatment. Doctors improvise like farmers. A drain, a clear tube with a spike at the end, is inserted into the leg. The piss, which makes the clear tube yellow, drips into a pitcher, like those in Kool-Aid advertisements, that sits beneath her bed.

Tired of living and afraid of dying, says Burned in the hall.

I please those in plaster shells, suspended by wire and sandbags, provide invalid's graffiti, sign my name to thighs and arms, write an obscenity behind a knee.

Hawkeye says, Go on, kiss her.

White shells creak as their occupants dig with back scratchers into crevices, around shrunken limbs, attacking healing itch.

Hawkeye's mother beckons, rattles the bottle of clear fluid that hangs on a hook, opens her arms.

It runs in the family: even dying's a spectacle. But I

approach, not understanding the necessity of a child's blessing. There's a steady but weak yellow current in the tube pinned to the bed.

Hawkeye smiles: it's the best he can do.

I take a step toward the open arms, feel my foot touch something, the pitcher, hear glass break on the cement floor, see the leg start, the old woman's anxious eyes. Spike rips flesh. The tube looks like a rising thermometer: piss gives way to red mercury, blood. I reach to pinch it off, to stop the flow, but Hawkeye slaps my hand.

Later, in the car, the green Chevrolet, Burned says, There's always something. No one ever dies right.

I look for facts.

"No one ever dies right."

Horse-T brings her to the shack. She's tall, deeply tanned, fleshly. I like her smile.

"Look me up in Sears," I hear her say to Horse-T. "I'm in the girdle section."

I send Lophead for the catalogue.

"It's a summer job," she says.

Horse-T whispers in the other room. I stand next to the blanket door.

"Just go in there and give him a little loving," he says to her, "make him feel good."

I look for facts, think of insults.

She sits on a wooden chair, legs akimbo, propping herself with hands on the insides of her thighs.

"Hi!" she says to me.

Horse-T offers her wine, but she shakes her head.

I sit on the floor.

"What's your name?" I ask.

"Abbey," she says.

I see on her left arm small scabs.

"Go on," says Horse-T. "I'm not going to watch."

She takes off her shoes, wiggles her toes, touches them with one hand.

"What do you want?" she says.

"I want to get out of here," I say.

Horse-T groans.

I touch her leg, put my hand around her ankle. She doesn't seem to mind.

"Hey!" I scream at Horse-T. "Hey!"

Abbey swings one leg back and forth, her toenails tapping against the leg of the chair. Slight sounds cut, shrapnel in jellyfish brains.

"For Christ's sake," says Horse-T, "chant or something."

"You don't remember me?" says Abbey.

I shake my head.

"Holy, holy, hoe-o-lee," says Horse-T.

Abbey frowns, stops swinging her leg.

"If you want to go . . ." she says to me.

"Holy, holy, hoe-o-lee."

"Shut up!" I scream at Horse-T.

He shrugs and then begins again. He lights a cigarette, rocks back and forth, looks like a censer.

"Do you want to fuck?" asks Abbey. Where she stopped shaving, just above the knee, there's a faint sleeve of bleached hair.

Horse-T laughs.

"Go away!" I scream at him. "Go away!"

"Sure, Niles," he says, "anything you say."

I hear him laughing outside the shack, see his face at the window.

"Go away!"

His boots squeak in the sand.

"Don't look at me," I say to Abbey.

I can feel her hard nails against my scalp. She smiles

giddily, but stands with an easy grace and lifts her shift over her head. She sunbathes nude. Her body is the color of brown brick. I sit on the floor, watching her above me, her figure arched, swelling at the belly, her arms, face, and hair against the ashy aluminum ceiling. Her pants are stained at the crotch. She puts them on the floor and sits on the chair in front of me, her legs akimbo. Through the dark hair I see her open like prayerful hands, thin lips with lazy serrations.

"Look," she says, "if you want."

Breasts flatten, become broader as she leans against the chair. The dark hair between her legs is streaked with red, bleached by the sun. The lips are salty, the inside of the thighs smooth against my face. Gently she touches the back of my head, pulls my face against her. Somewhere in the center of her body, she pivots. I touch a leg, a tendon behind a knee, feel it squeak between my fingers. When she laughs, I can feel the opening contract against my lips. Forehead pushes against a bone, cheek becomes moist, brushes against the inside of her thigh. She leans forward, kisses my lips, tastes herself.

"That's nice," she says. "I like it."

I look at the Coca-Cola clock above the door.

"That's nice," she says.

Eardrum quivers, a noisy spasm. I want her. Horse-T hammers on the door.

"You done yet, Niles?" he screams. "You finished her off?"

Coca-Cola clock marks time. It has a red second hand like a lobster's feeler.

"Go away," screams Abbey. I feel her tighten against my lips.

She stands and turns. Moist flesh on the inside of her thigh quivers as she walks. Shack creaks. Horse-T leans against the door. I watch Abbey as she lies on my cot, ignoring the stains, the snakeskin markings.

"Don't tire her out too much," says Horse-T.

"Go away," I scream.

Horse-T laughs.

The whites of her eyes are a little jaundiced, but her nipples are dark red, tanned.

"We'll go swimming afterward," she says. "Cold water . . ."

I kiss her left arm, feel the small scabs, diminished rubies, against my lips. Months of blood rushes. Light brown hair around the tips of her breasts. Abbey sits on the cot, legs dangling from each side, as though she were sitting on a picnic bench. Breasts become sharp, pointed as she sits up. She bites, touches my mouth with hers, breathes into me. Warm air pushes into my chest, makes it swell.

Horse-T laughs.

Ribbed moist channel, so warm it surprises me. She swings back and forth, pushes herself against me, throws her legs over my back. I feel muscles slither beneath the skin, a tight ring.

"She didn't learn how to fuck out of a book," screams Horse-T. "What's taking you so long?"

She puts her arm over her eyes as though shielding herself from the sun, but it slides from her brow, over her head, dangles from the end of the cot. She laughs, pleased as I run into her. She dissolves inside.

Horse-T pounds on the door.

She looks surprised.

"Holy, holy, hoe-o-lee."

She goes for a swim, comes back dripping, tells me she goes to an eastern college. I become angry, show her Lophead's correspondence courses, try to impress her with the schematic of a Heath kit.

* * *

Days pass.

Sis says, Down! Down! Her girl friends stand in a circle, tittering, wanting to see. Down! she says, down, Niles! Eyes widen with disbelief. Down, Niles.

I've got him trained, Sis explains.

Down!

I drop down. Girls' eyes widen. They titter among themselves, whisper, point. I sit, smile, cock my head to one side like a calendar spaniel. Girl friends are impressed, Sis proud.

Roll over! Roll over!

A kick, quick and pointed: I have hard ribs. I roll over, sit up, lie down, play dead, try to impress with my expertise, demand applause.

Heel! Heel!

I trot.

Why do you do that? a girl friend asks.

He's my brother, says Sis.

"Shit," says Horse-T to a friend in the other room.

"What's wrong?" asks Friend.

"With who?" says Horse-T. "With him? He's just lame."

I dream of prowling through the dump, looking through the trash, doors from Good Humor trucks, bathtubs with lion's feet, sunflower shower heads. It took millions of years to perfect me. I'll pry open glove boxes with a jack handle, look for private letters, prophylactics wrapped in silver foil. In a million more I'll be a smooth drop of flesh.

"Most murders occur in the summertime when the temperature is between ninety-six and ninety-eight degrees."

* * *

I pack my things in a suitcase, take apart my cot, and use one leg as a club. Dishes, glasses, piñata light bulb shatter. Clothes rip, boxes overturn, spill filthy clothes onto the floor. Piss splashes. I rip Lophead's photographs, sheets of halftone sensuality, scatter the bits around the room. His needle snaps beneath my heel. Good spike's hard to find, says Lophead, now this is a good spike. Crystal scatters over the cement floor. A guitar case dances around the room, cheap pinewood pushing through its plastic skin, its velvet lining ripped and sagging. The Coca-Cola clock explodes: its gears and wheels run like roaches for the corners. I rip rag curtains from the windows, throw them into the pile of junk. Refrigerator overturns, belches rotten meat, molding bread, bottles, stale melon, limp vegetables. In the kitchen I find a knife, then slash clothes, letters, furniture. I break the mirror in the bathroom, spill empty aspirin bottles from the cabinet. I overturn beds, cut them with the kitchen knife, throw stained stuffing onto the floor. Chair turns a cartwheel, shatters a wooden wall.

Boots squeak in the sand.

Horse-T steps over broken dishes, a torn blanket, kicks a splintered piece of wood. He picks up an aluminum chair, sets it straight, sits on it. He nods. Short, quick movements.

I pick up the suitcase and walk through the door.

"I didn't touch anything of yours," I scream, "nothing of yours."

In the reddish air the sun is mounted like a cheap memorial. For a few hours after dark there are angry sounds from the shack, and every now and then someone runs down the beach, looking for me. When it's quiet, I bathe, watch the phosphorescent skeleton of the ocean, towel myself with a shirt out of the suitcase. Sand fleas, hopping over my face, wake me in the morning. I climb the rocks to the highway, and from there I see a yellow spot against the side of the shack. It's that Indian.

San Francisco

After business hours I wander in financial sections, among buildings the color of dirty ice. All of the night watchmen, who sit in lobbies, smoking cigarettes and staring through glass doors, have good wristwatches, chronometers, professional instruments made for pilots and deep-sea divers: seconds are counted as precisely as dollars. A newspaper, like a kite with a broken back, blows in the street.

The knife makes mouths with stainless steel tongues on her belly. Camp-meeting eyes, a bit of spinal cord hanging over the torso's ragged collar, a head with red hair rolling into a corner of a monastic room: in the bathroom I vomit in the tub. Through the window I can see hills serrated with rows of houses. Beneath my fingernails there are bits of pale, skin-colored grit.

Newspapers report a murder.

* * *

The office building has a sign near the entrance, MARCHER, DEMOLITION AND CONSTRUCTION. The glass covering the empty directory is broken, and in the corner of the lobby newspapers and the remains of sack lunches are pushed into a bedlike pile. The elevator seems to hang by drying tendons: I take the fire stairs. The halls are filled with stale silence. In one of them I turn and see in the dust a line of footsteps leading to my shoes. I check the newspaper, the want ad there, and begin to climb again.

"Now look here," says Salesman in an office filled with light dirtied by the window. That's some suit Salesman's wearing, but there's a hole in his shoe, and he's got something in it, a piece of cardboard, gray sock, or skin. His feet rest on a green trash can. "This is one safe business."

He means kids' encyclopedias, a door-to-door hustle. When he looks at the stain on the knee of my suit I hang the paper in front of it.

"That ain't blood, is it?" says Salesman.

"Chili," I say. "I been eating out of cans."

Salesman sighs: he's seen better prospects.

"Gambling's something I used to do," he says, cracking a knuckle on a cardshark hand, "and take it from me, buddy, this is safer."

My liver burns, but when I smile I show good teeth.

"Used to get beaten, cheated, insulted," he says. "You name it, it's happened to me. One time or another."

Salesman's a desperate man: he hires me.

"Here," says Salesman, pushing money across the desk, "get yourself a suit. You ain't selling shit in that rag of yours."

* * *

I break a broomstick, pick at splinters until an end is sharp, then search for a small opening. Esophagus? Larynx? Damp red hair hangs like a tail. I put Beethoven on the phonograph, parade around the room with the greasy, heavy stick.

Stop it, I think.

I can't stop it.

"Stop that fucking crying," I scream.

My apartment has one room, a skylight that looks like a glass pup tent, a bed, a desk, one window with a view of iron chimneys, dragon's nostrils, that breathe on the roof. The white linoleum floor is always covered with soot.

A green grip with brass studs leans against the wall next to the door.

"The girl who lived here before you left some things behind," says the landlord when I move in. He points at the grip. "She'll be back for them."

When he's gone I go through the bureau and find some of her underwear, a letter, a plastic case in which there are two tampons. There's only the first page of the letter, and part of that has been ruined, stained with circles made by the bottom of a wet glass. It has "Paris" written beneath the date, and it's addressed to Margo ("Dearest Margo . . .").

" . . . but they think of me as just another American piece of ass. When they're done they kick me out in the morning. They're not so good in the sack, either. It's all right, though. I'd probably do the same to them if I got the chance. Too bad I'm a late sleeper. . . ."

It's written on spiral-notebook paper, and where the page was ripped out there's a serrated edge.

The grip is locked.

* * *

In an apartment house hounds bray, bark, growl behind green doors. I've got my sample case and a new
suit. I knock on doors, disturb the dogs. At the end of
the hall where there used to be a light fixture there's a
cluster of wires like a large tarantula. Good morning,
madam, good morning. How fortunate I've found you
home. I've called on a matter of supreme urgency. Not
a moment to lose. May I be so bold as to ask if you have
children, and the ages of those on whom rests the heavy
burden of mankind's salvation? That's the pitch. Christ,
morning beer: I've got to piss. Open the door! Dogs
growl. When a woman comes down the stairs I pretend
I'm a cop, spend a moment looking for suspicious
marks, criminal's spore, a fingerprint or empty car-
tridge, play the part of a rat inspector: I'm all business.
Open up! I move toward the dark end of the hall, bang
on a green door there, become convinced I've found an
empty apartment, a little privacy.

Unzip, unzip. The sound echoes in the hall.

Piss splashes against the green door, collects in yellow
beads on my shoes. The highlight of the week: the dog
inside sniffs with renewed frenzy. He sees with his nose,
I think. Let him have a look. Get a little under the door
for him. He sniffs, points, uric acid dancing in his nose.

Night chain snaps, becomes taut, quivers. Through
the narrow opening I see a red face, stricken with hang-
over, bluish hair.

"Yes . . . ?"

Her eyes move down, look at what's between my
fingers. I turn quickly, leave a broken, splashy half circle, then grab my case, in which there are charts, statis-
tics, both undeniable and complete, and walk a step or
two with a staggered gait. Me? Madam! I trapped a rat,
big as a hog, bludgeoned him to death with my case.

Hero's smile. Bows to appreciative citizens. All in the service of this fair city, madam. Wasn't nothing to it. Except when he bit my hand, clear through to the bone. He jumped to my shoulder, came in for the kill, drawn to the jugular: I could feel his whiskers on my cheek. My footsteps echo in the empty hall. Now I wouldn't mind if you'd invite me in, pour me a little drink for my troubles, undress, buy a series of books for your children. If, perchance, you should be one of those unfortunates without the blessing of a child I'd be more than willing to assist in the handiwork of God. I can see you're an intelligent woman, one who understands the value of an education. Look at these charts! Children without an education . . . well, asylum inmates, on the average, have six years of schooling, rapists, eight, felons, eleven. It's all right there in black and white, number and letters. Do you realize the complexity of the processes now taking place in the center of the sun? Opposed, of course, to the simple ones of just ten years ago. Your encyclopedia, madam, is out of date. Street doors slam.

Refrigerators, their doors closed with rope girdles, slouch against brick walls, are surrounded with grease-stained shopping bags, overflowing trash cans. Bluish light filters through the clouds. Two fifty in my pocket.

Salesman's door is one in the old style, polished oak and frosted glass, and through it I can hear an affected voice, distinct pronunciation. It's one cut up from a police dispatcher's.

"Have you made arrangements? Arrangements?"

Salesman always speaks as though he had a cigar in his mouth, but the records have done some good: his mumble is now fluent.

"Will you travel by ship, train, or airplane . . . ship
. . . train . . . or airplane . . ."

Through the door I see his pale and smeared bulk
move toward the phonograph. The lesson ends.

"Got some advice for you," says Salesman.

I stand before him in my new suit.

"Don't waste time on young women," he says. "They
ain't interested yet. Got to get knocked up first." He
points a finger at me and smiles slyly. "They're only
good if they're horny."

"I been to the barber," I say.

"Yeah," says Salesman. "Your hair looks good, although that suit could be a little . . . well . . . well
. . . you know, flashier. Should have more sparkle. Get
yourself a blue shirt and a blue tie. And a tieclip. We
don't run on no soft-selling ideas."

Salesman looks through the dirty windows.

"I hope you have better luck than I did," says Salesman, his voice falling into the litany of lost prospects,
"because in all the years I worked those fucking buildings I only got one stinking blow job."

A cockroach with a prehistoric shell, the color of to-
bacco juice, walks across my wall. I turn on the stove,
hold a pin with a bit of paper, put the tip between the
blue and yellow flames, wait until it glows like a small
soldering iron. Cockroach begins to run, his ancient
shell seesawing quickly: he knows what's coming.
Brothers told him, radio cockroaches that follow me on
my rounds, report on my whereabouts. Shell hisses,
bubbles, gives up hot brown juice. Pads lose traction.
Jesus, it stinks. Like burning electrical insulation. I drop
the pin on the Formica counter and think, It ain't doing
any good. There's a new generation every thirty-two
days.

I bring from the hardware store white powder to put around the stove and icebox, in the corner of the kitchen cabinets. With the handle of a spoon I slip some into sanctuaries, private cracks, favorite hiding places. Under the sink there are piles of transparent, shiny egg sacs. White powder makes the roaches thirsty: in the morning I find them in the toilet drinking themselves to death. Some are split up the middle like small bear-skin rugs.

Margo's about five and a half feet tall, has small, firm breasts, red hair, green eyes, freckles, a heart-shaped ass. She works for a company on the waterfront that imports tea and rugs. Her hair is its natural color unless she uses dye between her legs, too. She tells me that at work they sent some rugs to a department store where a woman, in the basement, unrolled one and was bitten by a cobra.

"I can't stand the smell of tea," says Margo.

She knocks on the door of my apartment.

"Hello," she says, "I hope I'm not disturbing you. I used to live here and I'm afraid I left some things behind."

I'm available smile.

"Oh, there it is," she says, "that's what I'm after."

She points at the green leather grip.

"There may be some old things in one of the drawers," she says. "Just throw them out. I don't need them any more."

She picks up the grip and hesitates for a moment at the door, but I don't invite her in: I'm embarrassed by quart beer bottles that stand like bloated chess pieces on the table behind the door.

"My name's Margo," she says.

She shrugs, turns to walk down the stairs, but I stop her with a joke. About cockroaches.

She laughs and says, "Come and see me. Here's my new address."

She hands me a slip of paper.

"We'll go out or something."

She walks sideways down the stairs so she can turn and smile.

There wasn't anything beneath my fingernails, no flesh, skin, pale grit. I haven't got a nail file, and I didn't clean them. In the bathroom I search through the medicine chest for a nail file, look around the toilet, behind the door, on the windowsill, under the bathtub with lion's feet, but I only find chips of paint, stains that look like crude maps.

I can't listen to Beethoven. Chamber music.

"I want to be left alone," I say. "I didn't do anything."

I try my neighborhood, knock on doors, hustle a little brain damage for the kids, but no one's buying. Ten A.M.: time for a break. Bell rings, warns the delicatessen man, who looks like a president. A protector of hams and cheese.

"Quart of beer," I say.

President must have cut his hand: I see a spot of blood. Sliced finger garnish for the ham. Silver discs roll and quiver on the marble counter. No, I think, my shirt wasn't stained. I've still got two. One I wash in the sink at night. If I'd stained a shirt I would have thrown it away.

President takes the quarters and goes to a cabinet meeting behind the cases of cat food.

But I could have bought another. Another shirt.

I see them across the street from the delicatessen, on

the steps of the church, sitting like fans in bleachers. Their jaundiced eyes follow as I carry the beer under my arm like a football. Fans are taking the cure: pants rolled to knees, exposing white skin with scabs and boils to weak sunlight. Each rests with a posture established by the years' discomfort. One wheezes through smashed nostrils, another sleeps with his mouth open, revealing teeth with dark holes, as though they'd been burned with a cigarette. I do a little soft-shoe for them, step into the gutter, bounce for a moment on a half-burned mattress there, and cross the street. One of them comes from the church, his arms, in the sleeves of his black coat, moving like a crab. Two or three fans have spread snot rags on the steps to dry along with their legs. Sidewalk's cracked, marred by small earthquakes.

"Hey," says Black Crab, "com'ere. I want to talk to you."

Scarlet face, black beard. Newspapers are stuffed into his overcoat, a brown bag into his broken fly.

"I'm talking to you," he says.

"So what?"

"A hard guy," he says, gesturing toward the other fans. "You hear him?"

Black Crab looks at the plastic tag on my case in which Salesman has written in elaborate script, *Mr. Niles Cabro.*

"What you got in the case, Niles?" says Black Crab.

"What's he got in his pockets," says a fan, "is more like it."

"Come on," says Black Crab, "help us out on a bottle."

I shake my head.

"Your fingernails are dirty, Niles," says Black Crab, "you know that?"

"What's he got in his pockets?" says a fan.

I look for a place to drink the beer and find some steps leading down below a stoop, toward the basement door. Got to keep the suit clean, I think, spreading the bag's brown paper over one of the stairs. Salesman was more desperate than I thought: seven days and I'm into him for a hundred bucks. Two bucks in my pocket: carfare to a more likely part of town, three quarts so I can sleep, a can of chili. I feel cold cement through the paper. Beer bottle plays the steps like a xylophone, collapses next to the basement door.

Black Crab makes mechanical motions from the church, hails me as I pass.

"Hey," he says, "I know you. I seen you. I remember."

"What happened to the last fifty I advanced you?" says Salesman.

I can see some printing in the hole: he must have changed his cardboard just this morning.

I shrug and say, "Maybe there's something wrong with the pitch."

"There ain't anything wrong with the pitch!" shouts Salesman. "You better sell some books, boy, or you're going to find your ass in a sling."

"How am I going to sell books," I say, "if I'm hungry?"

Salesman's a modest man: he's ashamed when he reaches for his wallet, as though he were taking down his pants. The wallet's a large one with hidden compartments and zippers.

"Keep your nails clean," says Salesman, giving me ten dollars. "Lot of people particular about that. You don't want to look like a junkie."

Me? Oh, no, not me. I only use it for medicinal pur-
poses.

"Get yourself a nail file."

At the end of the block the N. Judah waits. Electricity
hums in the wires. Streetcars huddle together in the
square like cows in a corral. Monetary music, change in
the coffee grinder box. Crowded streets, hats, faces,
coats, papers, arms swirl together like the specks of a
color-blindness test. The streetcar rocks back and forth,
a rolling barge on Market Street. The black man across
from me has a toothpick the shape and color of a nose
ornament carved from bone. I study my fingernails,
then climb down from the N. Judah and watch it move
away like a green insect, scaled with windows and
doors, its feelers reaching for electricity.

I sit in the living room and look out the window at the
hills serrated with rows of houses. Margo's apartment is
almost monastic. White walls, solid dark furniture, the
damp smell of plaster. But there are light colors, a thick
rug with an intricate pattern, a fireplace, and in her
bedroom there's a large brass bed. Margo wears a green
dress that sets off her hair and eyes.

"I didn't think you were going to come around," she
says, smiling, handing me a drink, stepping close
enough to press me into the aura of sheets dried in the
open air.

"I don't know anyone in the city," I say.

She laughs and sits in a chair opposite me, crossing
her legs at the ankle.

"Well," she says, "I don't know how good I'm going to
be. As far as introducing you to people goes. The
women I know would try to take you away, and the
men would be jealous."

"That's all right," I say. "I've been a little lonely."

She frowns, has a sip of her drink, and says, "What's in there?"

My case. I've been reading those books at night: Caesar, fossils, records of basic slime, Madame Curie, the Black Death.

"So?" she says, eyeing the case as though it were something she had to clean up with a paper towel.

"You don't understand," I say. "I want to sell them. The books."

"Sure," she says.

"I do," I say.

"Okay!" she says with a got-another-live-one smile. "I believe you."

She teases the edges of her lips with a few strands of hair.

"Where you from?"

I tell her stories of the East Coast, New York, the Village, summers in Europe, a family with more money than is good for it, an unhappy year at Harvard.

"Where's Harvard?" she says.

I hesitate for a moment, and she laughs.

"It's all right, Niles. If that's your name. You can tell me whatever you want. It really doesn't matter."

Bay windows protrude like fat bellies from the front wall of my building. Behind the street door there's a woman who seems to grow noticeably older between morning and night. I stand next to her, convinced I should be able to hear her creaking flesh.

"Hello!" I say, but it does no good: age has turned words into noise. She holds the end of a clothesline leash while her dog, a black-and-white mongrel, squats in the gutter, quivers while he makes his stool, then runs between the trash cans. She remains inside, know-

ing how vulnerable she is, frightened by a drop of water, an evil wind, smoking a cigarette with a slow and
careful elegance, letting the smoke drift in a steady
wisp from her lips to her nose. Eyes should age, too, I
think, should grow into transparent prunes, should
have cataracts like small icicles. The old woman looks at
me with some confusion: was I the young man who
lived there ten, fifteen, twenty years ago? That nice one
who walked her dog, who helped her with her grocer-
ies (although God knows the bags get lighter every
year)? Or that one the police took away one night? She
looks away from me and reels in the black-and-white
mongrel (she's ten dogs old, a private reckoning), hand
over hand, as though she were sounding the street's
depth.

In the small market on the corner the Chinese grocer
argues with his wife, ignores the tinkling of the bell
when I open the door. They titter at one another, make
accusative gestures, move their heads up and down,
point at the cash register. The grocer becomes so angry
he speaks Chinese to me. Three quarts, a can of chili, a
package of cigarettes: broke.

The old woman lies at the foot of the stairs, her house
dress above her knees: it must have opened like an
umbrella as she fell. I see white skin, a map of bluish
veins. Her head rests on the landing, a heavy footworn
piece of slate. The dog runs up and down the hall, licks
at the blood that's splattered here and there, matted in
gray hair. The woman tries to cover herself, the traces
of schoolgirl hair on her legs.

"My head," she says. "I'm afraid to move. . . ."

I smooth the dress over her legs.

"Clothesline leash . . ." she says. Someone runs up
the stairs, pounds on a door, asks for a telephone. Her

eyes are a smoky, diluted color ". . . got tangled up
. . . I fell. . . ."

Professional mourners, police cars and ambulances,
wail beyond the door. Dog quivers, whines, pisses on
the floor beside the woman, then runs up the stairs.

"I remember you," she says, "I remember."

Firemen, in all-weather gear, looking like displaced
seamen, come through the door with axes and crow-
bars. On the floor, around the woman's head, there's a
corona of flame-shaped stains.

Through my window I can see a serrated skyline,
buildings of differing height, enlarged gravestones. On
the roof a junkie holds a spike protected by a Lindy pen
top: he wants to be safe when he carries the point in his
pocket. Through the wall I can hear the lunatic piano
player composing his new music, a score for the asylum.
Tinkle-tinkle-thump-thump.   Tinkle-tinkle-thump-
thump. I bang on the wall with a tin pot, but it doesn't
do much good: inmates hesitate in an idiots' dance,
piano player begins again.

"Stop that!" I scream. "Stop that goddamned piano
playing!"

Soot covers the floor like a thin black carpet.

"You'll have to get used to that," says Margo, standing
in my door, holding the green grip. "He almost drove
me mad."

I drink the second quart of beer, cook chili, make a
cockroach trap out of the can, wait with a pin in the
bluish light from the stove. White powder, white curse.
I find offspring with legs on one side only, turning in an
unbreakable circle, their shells as convoluted and
crusted as a walnut, some of them so brittle they shatter
at quick movement. All of the roaches drag behind a

long and waxy tail that looks like the tip of a penpoint holder.

With my case I walk the streets of Chinatown, watch the dragon dancing among parked cars, beneath nautical fire escapes, through spectators standing on the sidewalks. Chinese girls smile. I flinch at firecrackers, smell their acrid, lingering odor. The dragon, wearing twenty pairs of shoes, makes serpentine movements through the crowd.

"You ain't selling shit in Chinatown," says Salesman. "They ain't buying. Most of them don't speak English anyhow."

I knock on doors. A rug salesman has gone before me: half the buildings have the same cheap carpet with a rosy pattern. Good afternoon, madam, good afternoon. I sell books. A complete set to a senile woman who never had children. I pray while Salesman deposits the check.

"I'll be goddamned," says Salesman. "It's good."

I watch desperation stalk desperation, see a woman dancing at the top of a lighted pole. I go inside, get a drink, watch the women (COLLEGE COEDS, reads a poster, girls from the university across the bay). Pocahontas, her hair in braids, dances to a wino band. I sit up front, unashamed, watch her breasts move up and down. In the last row well-practiced hands move carefully beneath overcoats spread on laps. But Pocahontas ignores them. Across the bay someone is raped. In the last row they are silent, intent on their business. I walk the streets, look for suspicious stains. Back row men must bring something to clean their pants. Limpers move up and down the street, amazed by the agility of women dancing at the tops of lighted poles.

* * *

Salesman's come up with a new idea.

"If they haven't got the money," he says, "why you just give 'em one of these."

His office is filled with black plastic banks, each shaped like a mortarboard.

"Tell 'em it's just twenty-five cents a day, tell 'em to stop smoking, tell 'em anything."

I nod, put a couple of banks in my case.

"And keep those fingernails clean," says Salesman.

I drop the case, put my hands in my pockets.

"Listen," says Salesman sympathetically, "the old foot in the door thing ain't that bad. Lot to be said for it."

He gives me the old elbow in the ribs and laughs.

"You look nervous, boy," he says. "They keeping you busy?"

"Don't come in me," says Margo, "don't come in me."

Mose Allison sings it: I hum along. Pipes belch and clank, water runs in the wall. Her face is surrounded by a corona of red hair: we make love with the light on, listen to the joints of the brass bed squeak. There's an injury lurking in my seminal tubes.

"Did you do that?" she says, sitting on the drops, feeling them spread beneath her buttocks. "Is that all you?"

"I'm sorry," I say.

"It's all right," she says.

"We can change the sheets."

"It's all right," she says.

I rip the sheets, pull them from the bed, roll them into a ball, and throw them in a corner.

"For Christ's sake," she says, rolling on the floor.

I search through her linen closet.

"Here they are," I scream, "here they are. All nice and clean!"

I hold clean sheets like thick, heavy semaphores.

The bathroom door is open a little and I can hear her urinate into the porcelain bowl. Her clothes are scattered on the floor, mixed with mine. I search for something to wear, stoop over dark cloth, feel semen stuck on my leg, her moisture in my pubic hair. I hold her skirt to my face for a moment, feel a genuine and deep affection for her. The bathroom door opens, and her shadow falls across the bed, clothes, floor.

"What are you doing?" says Margo.

I shake my head.

"What are you?" she says, grabbing the skirt. "You were smelling it."

"No," I say, "that's not . . ."

The door slams.

We sit in the kitchen, at a blue table with white chairs, and have a drink.

"You shouldn't have done that," says Margo matter-of-factly. "You spoiled a good time."

I get drunk, feel my liver burn, tell her that I love her.

"No one's played that since yesterday," says Margo, pointing to the phonograph. "Why don't you put a record on?"

A knife with a serrated blade sits on the counter.

In the aquarium I stand in the dark rooms, move from window to window. Luminous fish swim from wall to wall. A large shark sleeps near the bottom of his tank. I walk between pipe railings, read inscriptions printed in white, recessed letters on sheets of black plastic, chant to myself in solemn tones Latin names.

"Do you like the aquarium?" says Margo. "We could go. Some afternoon."

Eels move through the water as though made of silk. An octopus sits like a lump of brown rubber, his tentacles covered with toy-arrow suction cups. A stingray glides through the water like a rubber jet. Limpers move between the aisles. I bump into someone, feel firm breasts flatten against my forearm.

"I'm sorry," I say, "excuse me."

"It's all right," says Margo.

Crabs crawl over rocks, make their pincers work. A school of silver fish dive quickly: it looks as though someone has dropped a handful of nickels into the tank. Shuffling feet, quiet voices. A fish library.

"Hey, mister," says a boy. He pulls my sleeve. "I can't see. Can you hold me up?"

I lift him to my shoulders, put his legs around my neck, hold him by his ankles. He puts his hands around my forehead like an Indian band. I point out a small seahorse with a serrated spine.

"He likes you," says Margo.

The boy follows shyly from tank to tank.

I hear bars rattle and through the bathroom window I see a face, its eyes measuring me.

"There's nothing here to steal," I scream. "I broke in myself."

Tinkle-tinkle-thump-thump.   Tinkle-tinkle-thump-thump. I open a quart of beer, wait for a cockroach, and think, In a minute I'm going right through that wall. I'll strangle the bastard if he doesn't stop.

"I'm setting you a quota, boy," says Salesman, "and by God you better meet it."

I stand at the reference desk of the library, finally ready to ask for the back issues of the paper, for reports of murder, but when the clerk asks me what I want, I shake my head and walk out of the building.

The druggist looks at me as though I wanted to buy something without a prescription.

"A nail file," I say, "give me a nail file."

I listen to Beethoven, see viscera as gray as wet newspaper, blood-clot leeches clinging to the torso. The open neck gives up the broomstick with a sucking sound. I lift by damp red hair something that's as heavy as a bowling ball to the kitchen table and wrap it with newspapers. A clean, dry package. I smash the record on the phonograph, clean myself in the bathroom, put the package in a paper sack.

Fishing birds, black slits in the sky, swirl over flotsam. I stand at the ferry's rail as it moves across the bay, toward the aquarium. The whistle blows. Steam escapes from the brass valve on the smokestack and dissolves into blue sky. I carry the package in a brown paper sack. On the sunny side of the ferry the rail is lined with men, women, children. The engines throb below, make the boards of the deck vibrate. Some of the passengers ride inside, behind glass, and I can see their silent lips move. A deckhand looks at me suspiciously.

The whistle opens the air. At the end of the deck a tourist points a camera at his family, two young girls, a boy, his wife. The wife looks over her shoulder, sees me at the rail, the sack in my hand. She frowns: the picture will be ruined. The bench is wet with spray, but I sit on it, not wanting to be in the background.

Sea birds funnel over the sack for a moment before it sinks.

"We'll buy some popcorn," says Margo. "You throw it on the water and the gulls eat it."

I think of scuba divers, like spacemen, swimming in the channel. They took another photograph. The tourists. Caught the sack as it flew from the deck.

"I've always liked the ferry," says Margo. "Don't you?"

"Excuse me."

I look up. The tourist, in a long, eastern coat, stands before me.

"Excuse me," he says, "but could you take a photograph of all of us together?"

He gestures toward his family. They huddle against the rail, smile, nod their heads.

"I'll focus it and everything," he says. "All you have to do is push this button. Here." A crooked finger points at the small button on top of the camera.

"Sure," I say.

We walk up the deck together.

"Just out from Philly," he says. "Ever been there?"

"No," I say. No. I never have been. No.

I shake my head.

"All right," he says to his family. "Get closer together now. Little closer."

Family huddles together. I look over the water, try to hide my face. Husband peers through the camera. Wife smiles at me.

"Okay," he says. "Just stand there and push the button. Wait for me to get around."

He runs to his family, puts his arm around them, smiles. I see them through the shaking lens.

"Thank you," says the wife. "Thank you ever so much."

"Sure," I say.

Family dissolves. Girls look at birds.

"Thank you," says the husband.

I nod, smile, turn away.

"Hey, mister," says the boy. "What did you throw in the water?"

Brown eyes. He smiles, swings back and forth on the railing.

"I didn't throw anything into the water," I say to him quietly.

"Yes you did," he says, swinging back and forth. "I saw you."

I feel my smile. Engines throb.

"I didn't throw anything," I say, patting him on the back.

"Yes you did," says the wife. "I saw you, too."

Sun flashes off windows. Papers, trash, blow up the deck.

I shake my head.

"Come on, children," says the wife, "come on."

She gathers them together, ushers them down the deck. She looks over her shoulder at me, whispers to her husband. He looks, too, and then they disappear around the front of the ferry.

"You did, too," screams the boy, running for a moment back onto the deck. "You did, too!"

The wife grabs him.

Engines throb. Passengers eat popcorn, put nickels into telescopes with meters. Gulls hover over a patch of white water the size of a manhole cover.

"You ain't selling worth a shit, Niles," says Salesman. "You ain't getting any action."

My replacement, a balding adolescent, stands in the hall.

"You're through," says Salesman, pointing at me with

a cardshark finger. "Here's twenty-five bucks. That's my vacation money."

I hope he spends his fucking vacation on a streetcar. Twenty-five bucks!

"Get out," he screams. "Beat it!"

"Have you made arrangements?" I say. "Arrangements?"

"I was good to you, Niles," screams Salesman, "and this is what I get. . . ."

He ain't ever had a vacation, I think; first one's going to be in a pine box.

"Leave the case here," says Salesman.

I take the N. Judah, walk up the block, go into the bar across the street from my building. Green doors, stained-glass window, a sign in old-fashioned pink neon tubing, a long elbow-polished bar. Cross-eyed bartender brings me a drink, but she doesn't charge for it. Christ, I think, it's true. Salesman was good to me.

I order another drink.

"You don't have to give it away," I say. "Here."

I put a properly wrinkled five-dollar bill on the bar.

I'll send Salesman the suit. Maybe my replacement can have it cut down to size.

Shit!

"What's that?" asks the bartender.

"Nothing."

"Niles," she says, "I know you're in there."

She knocks again.

"Who is it?" I say.

"Margo," she says.

I think for a moment of running across the roof, hiding behind a chimney, climbing down the fire escape.

"Open up," she says.

Landlord's a scavenger: whenever a building is torn

down, he's there, digging through debris, looking for locks. The one on my door is old and sticky, a three-time loser, veteran of the great earthquake and fire. I hammer at the door, rattle the lock, try to remember its special temperament.

"Why haven't you called me?" says Margo, stepping into my apartment, sniffing the rancid air. A brown dress clings to her firm, tight figure. Heavy hair, a silk scarf. She smiles, runs her tongue over my lips, pulls on me with her comfortable weight.

"Why haven't you?" she says.

I hold up a hand, let her see the quarter moon of blood beneath each nail: I've used the file. She goes to the bed and begins to undress. Her stockings make an electric crackle as she takes them off, spreading her fingers beneath the sheer material. She holds them to the light for a moment before dropping them on the floor.

"Oh, come on," she says, "don't be so moody."

She sits at the edge of the bed, feet and knees together, hands at her sides, her nipples becoming sharp and distinct in the cold air.

"I thought I touched you," I say.

"Not recently," she says with a laugh.

I kiss her body, bite her toes, fingers, run my tongue along her thigh, between her legs. Her skin, carroty hair, breasts quiver through salty water.

"I didn't, though," I say.

"What?" she says, sitting up, looking at my eyes.

I bite her along her ribs, make her laugh, giggle. She sees the blood beneath each nail. I touch a breast, a nipple that has the color and shape of a pencil eraser. She watches the hand.

"What?"

"I didn't touch you."

She hides behind her body, watches my hands and eyes.

"Like this?" she says, pushing my hand against an open thigh.

I shake my head.

"With a knife."

"I see," she says.

"I've been frightened," I say with a shrug. "I couldn't go outside."

She stuffs her underwear into her purse, then moves toward her dress in a slow and careful manner: she doesn't want me to start raving.

"I'm sorry," she says.

I listen to her rustling dress, make her start when I help her with the zipper.

"Do you need money?" she says.

I shake my head.

"Here," she says, digging in her purse, "here's twenty. You'll need it."

She leaves the bill on the table and steps quietly out the door.

It takes about a week after I drop a postcard to Horse-T. He comes into the bar across the street from my building.

"How you been?" he says, touching my elbow.

"Fine."

"You look it," he says.

One of my hands hides in a pocket.

"Ain't you glad to see me?" he asks.

"My Indian," I say. "You still got it?"

"Sold it," says Horse-T. "Three hundred and fifty bucks. Got it right here." He pats his pocket. "Had to change things around some and register it as an 'assembled,' right? And . . ."

"Give it to me!"

Horse-T counts out three hundred and fifty dollars. It's a heavy pile of money.

"That's right, Niles," he says, "keep it up. They're going to plug you into the wall."

Cross-eyed woman sees the money and brings the bottle over.

"What you been doing?" says Horse-T. "Juicing it every day? You got Chinese eyes. Yellow."

Horse-T pulls the corners of his eyes, makes them slant.

"Flied lice," he says, "flied lice. Ha! Ha! Pretty funny."

"I'm glad to see you," I say. "I am."

"Good," he says. "Glad to hear it."

Bartender looks at the money.

"You didn't kill somebody to get it, did you?" she says to me.

"Yeah," I say, "a bartender."

She laughs.

"Listen, Niles," says Horse-T, "I got our Ford outside. I'm going home. . . ."

Home. If I move I'll break into a thousand pieces. Bartender will sweep me up, push me into the dust bin. Bits of crystallized bone will dance along the floor.

"You know," says Horse-T, "Oregon."

"Oregon," I say, nodding, "Oregon."

I can smell Farmer, a rank bastard, hiding in the lining, can feel him on the door handle. He smiles, greets me. I lie in the back while Horse-T drives.

"We'll be there tomorrow night," says Horse-T. "Ain't nothing to it."

"Roll up the window," I say.

"Sure, Niles," says Horse-T.

Drive shaft purrs beneath me, pushes its warmth through the floorboards. We pass hills serrated with rows of houses.

Southeastern Oregon

"Shhh," I say.

Horse-T swaggers, kicks skeletal weeds, makes breast-stroke motions through the brush. I stand like a big-game hunter, listening to his careless sounds, waiting for him to make the top of the ridge.

"Shhhh," I say.

"Shhhh up your ass," he says.

He moves along the ridge, a fluid hump against the stars. Tire iron swings next to my leg. Those stars are so thick I feel the sky's depth, my prehensile, creature-like nature. Some chalky, bone dust, others sharp, like a piece of black paper with pinholes held to the light.

I carry the tire iron.

"Don't make so much noise," I say.

At the end of the ridge, where it levels off, there's a shed. That's where we want to go, but she's sitting right up there in the house, not fifty yards away. I can see the house, the orange curtains, jack-o'-lantern light filling the yard. She's sitting up there in the front room. I walk in the gully, but it's noisy there, too.

Horse-T holds the shed's lock in his hand, rattles it against the iron bracket. The lock is old, looks like something out of Jiminy Cricket.

"Shit," he says, "it's locked."

"She knows," I say.

"How's that?" asks Horse-T.

"This is the first time the shed's been locked," I say, "and anyway, she's pissed off."

I hold the tire iron under Horse-T's nose.

"That's why I brought this along."

Wood screeches as it gives up the bracket. Horse-T stops me as I begin to throw it into the brush.

"Leave it here, Niles," he says. "Somebody'll put it back on."

She's sitting up there in the front room. It doesn't matter to me. I just wanted to throw it, that bracket.

"Ain't she?" I ask as we stand over the box on the floor of the shed.

Horse-T takes a flashlight off the workbench and snaps it on. They're packed in sawdust.

"Ain't she pissed off?" I ask.

They look like flares, packed in sawdust.

"Sure she is," says Horse-T. "What do you think?"

He gives me the light and leans over the box.

"She wouldn't try to stop us, would she?" I say. "Seeing as how she knows."

"She's already tried," he says. He stops taking them out of the box and points outside, toward the bracket. "But you notice," he says, "she didn't try real hard."

He smiles at me, then goes back to the box, carefully picking them out. I can't hear anything, except Horse-T's fingers digging in the sawdust, against the side of the box.

"They're soft," says Horse-T, fingering one of them.
"So what?" I ask.
"Nothing," says Horse-T.
I don't ask about her losing the place.
"Except," says Horse-T, "we're liable to blow the shit out of ourselves."
He fingers them carefully, lines them up on the floor, counts them. He stands, takes from the bench a pair of pliers, a roll of fuse, a small cardboard box.
"Formula's broken down," he says. "They got soft spots. Formula breaks down into nitro. Here."
He hands me the box. Something rattles inside. I open it and see the blasting caps, each looking like a silver bullet.
"Put those in your pocket," he says.
I carry the fuse; it's round and smooth like a new piece of telephone wire.

And she's right up there in the house. Horse-T's mother. She's frightened and angry.
The flat landscape is marked by her house, one story, four rooms, surrounded by a defense of unfinished chores, unmended machines, a rusted harrow, hand tools, treadless tires, spools of barbed wire half burrowed in the sandy earth. Horse-T's quiet when we drive up to it the first time. I park our Ford and Farmer in the front yard, thinking, after I get out of the car, it looks like this Ford has always been here. All Horse-T says is, This is it. But back up the road when I roll down the window and whistle at the sheep, Horse-T laughs and says, They ain't run that hard since I left. But when we drive into the yard, he's quiet. She stands at the kitchen window, watching us, Ford.
So you've come home, she says.

*　*　*

The left side of my shirt droops, weighed down by the box of caps. I put the pliers in my back pocket. Horse-T follows me up the gully, slips, grunts, falls. I hear his body hit the sandy bottom. The sticks roll away from him. Like blind men after spilled pencils, we crawl in the gully, following our fingers.

"Easy, Niles," says Horse-T. "Don't you go stepping on them."

She's tried to fix her house up, too. It embarrasses Horse-T, but he wants me to see it anyway. She saved egg cartons made of purple fiber, those boxes with three spaces for eggs along one side and four along the other. She saved them, sprayed them with gold paint, and stapled them to the ceiling like acoustical tile.

Look at that, says Horse-T. Shit!

He points to the ceiling and laughs, but he's watching me all the same.

Ain't nothing wrong with it, I say, you don't have to laugh.

There's a knitted cover for the telephone.

We find one and then another. Our knees squeak in the sand.

"Goddamn, goddamn," says Horse-T. "This is something you just don't do."

I find one behind a rock, another in the brush. I won't turn on the light: that would be asking too much of her. We kneel next to each other, make a rake of four hands. We find three more. Horse-T counts them.

"There's one more," he says, his arms filled with small red logs.

I find it under my heel.

* * *

Niles! Oh, Niles, she says when I come into the
kitchen. She holds her hands beneath her breasts. You
frightened me, she says.

We both turn our backs, pretend it didn't happen.
She doesn't hear me at the sink. But later, I see her in
the storage room off the kitchen, a clapboard addition
with a freezer door. She drinks vodka. It is a large bottle, so heavy she has to drink out of it with a straw.

I'm sorry, Niles, she says, strangers in the house make
me nervous.

What did she say to you? asks Horse-T later, in our
room.

Nothing, I say.

I'm asking you something, Niles, he says angrily.

Strangers, I say, she said it was strangers in the house.

He looks toward the wall through which we can hear
her knocking pots and pans together, insisting on her
presence.

"You hear that?" asks Horse-T. He crouches in the
shadow of a bailer, a flat, tanklike machine. Orange
light fills the yard. Horse-T cocks his head toward the
road. I stop, hearing the caps rattle in their box.

"Somebody's out by the road," he says.

"I didn't hear anything," I say.

The curtains in the front room of the house open
quickly, allow white light to fall across the yard. She
stands at the window, looking toward the road, her
breath fogging the glass. A hand rests against the middle sash.

"See," says Horse-T, "she heard it, too."

She's short, dressed in a brown dress with a full skirt.
Farm-scarred face, hair colored with mail-order dye.

"I didn't hear anything," I say.

Curtains drop together, sway back and forth for a moment like a woman's long skirt.

"If she heard it," says Horse-T, "somebody's there."

Horse-T and I move past the house, down the gravel drive to the car, the road. It's a nice new Buick with spaceship controls, dark-green gauges with orange needles, the color of spacemen's blood. I take the sticks from Horse-T, lay them gently on the floor behind the front seat.

In the kitchen I look out the window and I know it has nothing to do with strangers being in the house. Beyond the glass there is flat land, marked only by a road that leads to the horizon, land clipped by prehistoric sky. Scalloped telephone wire. It's a child's stick drawing. Three lines.

I'm sorry, I say to her.

It's okay, she says, closing the freezer door. An alcohol rush.

Horse-T nudges me. Against the stars I see the outline of the hood of the car, two figures leaning on it. One has a bottle tipped to his lips.

"No need to bring anyone along," I say quietly to Horse-T.

"Shit," says Horse-T. "That you, Dink?"

"Yeah," says Dink. "I heard you been back."

When I open the door I can see by the dashlight Dink's face is pocked.

"For Christ's sake," says Horse-T, "shut the door. She ain't blind."

Dink's tall, about six three, and heavy, too. He wears overalls, a blue shirt beneath them. He smiled when I noticed the pocks.

Dink passes the bottle over to Horse-T. The other figure doesn't move.

"Who's that?" asks Dink, gesturing toward me with the bottle.

"That's Niles," says Horse-T, "Niles Cabro. From Hollywood."

"Yeah?" says Dink, stepping toward me. "Is that right?"

He offers me his muscle-swollen hand. He seems at ease because my hands are large, too.

The other figure doesn't move.

"That right?" asks Dink. "You ever meet any movie stars?"

"Sure," I say. "Lots. This hand has touched Jayne Mansfield."

"That right?" asks Dink.

He looks at the hand.

"She's dead," says the figure who leans against the car.

"Oh, he's a mean mother-fucker," says Horse-T. "You better look out for him, Niles."

All I can see of him, the man who leans against the car, is an even, clean profile. He speaks into the air before him, not bothering to look toward us.

"You know any other?" Dink asks. He says it without viciousness. A good-natured curiosity I don't mind satisfying.

"I raced Steve McQueen on Mulholland."

"Steve McQueen, shit."

"Merrit," says Dink, "you are the most unfriendly bastard I've ever seen."

"Steve McQueen, shit," says Merrit again.

Merrit's careful about the way he moves. He greets Horse-T, offers his hand.

"Don't mind him," Dink says to me. "He just wants to be in the movies."

I think of a farmhouse bedroom filled with fan magazines. Halftone glamour.

"What'd you put in the car, Niles?" asks Merrit.

"Nothing," I say.

Horse-T chuckles.

In the kitchen I hear her knocking pots and pans together, putting them on the stove. My clothes are damp, cold. On my hand I finger new blisters, small, pale domes. Horse-T chuckles.

She may be losing the place, he says, but she got herself a new car. That Buick right out there in the yard. Nothing she likes better than a new car, he says.

She comes through the door, hands us cans of beer. Horse-T was right about hard work. I load them. Horse-T sits behind a machine that cuts potatoes into small cubes, "seed." I load them all day onto the bed of the truck. Hundred-pound sacks. Horse-T chuckles behind the machine. I lift those sacks straight up. Horse-T brings the last one around, swings it back and forth, waits until it's about even with the bed, then knees it. Sack goes up easily.

That's the way you've got to do 'er, Niles, he says.

Thanks, I say, suddenly aware of the muscles in my face, but I like my way better.

Niles, he says, laughing, oh, Niles.

We sit in our beds opposite one another, like tired subway riders. Horse-T leans back, looks at the boxes on the ceiling.

I ask Horse-T about what's in the shed, and after he tells me, I ask him where we can use it.

Well, he says, there's a trestle . . . ain't really a trestle, but it looks like one.

I saw it, I say, when we came in. Over the road.

That's the one, says Horse-T.

It looks like a wharf on a South Pacific island. Long and black. It crosses a four-lane highway.

It really ain't a trestle, says Horse-T, it's got a big water pipe instead of tracks. Waters most of the farms around here.

He gestures toward the wall.

Well . . . I say.

Let me think about it, he says.

The light goes on as Merrit opens the door. A stretched schema of windows and doorposts spreads over the gravel shoulder of the road.

"It's all right," says Horse-T. "They might as well come along."

I'm not happy about it, but I understand his comfort with old hostility, habitual words. It'll be a short home-coming, I think.

"You remember the time," Dink says to Horse-T, "you remember . . ."

I look toward the house, see a shadow cross the curtain. Horse-T sees it, too.

"Anyway," says Horse-T to me as I climb into the back seat of the car, "we've got some time to kill."

"Sure," I say.

I lean back on the bed, feel an ache shaped like a saddle in the small of my back. Maybe, I think, I'll work harder tomorrow just to prove nothing vital's been broken.

How come, I say, leaning back, lighting a cigarette, blowing smoke toward the ceiling, how come we're working so fucking hard if she's going to lose the place anyway?

Horse-T takes a sweat-stained joint out of his shirt
pocket and lights it.

Even if we get that shit into the ground, I say, someone else is going to . . .

Horse-T pulls a small cloud of smoke out of the air,
like a cigarette commercial run backward.

Salty, says Horse-T, very salty. Smoking myself.

That's a lot of work, I say, especially when you . . .

You want to smoke a little of me? he asks, passing the
joint over.

Sure, sure, I say, anything to oblige.

Horse-T examines his arm carefully, flicks away dark
bits of dirt that are stuck to his skin. He rolls back on his
bed.

Look at those fucking egg boxes, says Horse-T, watching me. Just look at them.

He begins to chuckle. He's right. It's salty.

I hear a tight, cold sound like a freezer door being
closed. Dink and I sit in the back seat. Horse-T releases
the brake, waits for a moment, hoping the car will coast.
Flat land, too flat for any coasting, I think.

"You want a push?" I ask.

Horse-T starts the engine quickly, looks toward the
house, then fumbles with the lights. He turns on the
dashlight by mistake. Dink's got one pocked face.

"It ain't catching," says Dink to me, as he passes the
bottle. "Have a drink."

"Fucking new car," says Horse-T.

I drink palm-warmed bourbon.

"Thanks," I say.

"Sure," says Dink.

"What's that in the back seat?" asks Merrit.

"Nothing," I say.

"Looks like a little dynamite," says Merrit.

Horse-T pulls on the bottle, passes it to me.

"Right, right," says Horse-T.

Merrit shows us his clean profile, his smile. The greenish light from the dashboard tints his teeth. Stunted good looks. Just enough to be vain.

"You want to go to Hollywood?" I ask.

"No," he says.

Dink laughs. "Sure he does," he says. "He's lying."

"Niles?" asks Horse-T.

I reach for the bottle, feel it clublike in my hand.

"You want to go to Hollywood?" I ask.

Merrit shakes his head.

"Come on, Merrit," says Dink. "Who won the Academy Awards last year? He knows all of that shit."

"Shut up," says Merrit. "You're drunk."

"Fucking A," he says. "You just tell me who won those awards."

Horse-T lets the Buick drift in a corner. He likes the way it handles. Little better than Ford, but then it ain't got Farmor. A stick rolls across the floor, stops against the drive-shaft hump.

"He'd have a problem, though," Dink says to me.

"What?"

"If he went to Hollywood," says Dink.

"I'm not going anywhere," says Merrit.

"Tits," says Dink to me.

I hold the sticks against the wall of the car with my foot. "Tits," I say. I nod.

"But he's been working on that," says Dink.

Horse-T laughs.

"You still working on it, Merrit?" asks Dink.

Merrit says nothing.

"Come on," says Dink. "Say something, you unfriendly bastard."

Merrit turns in his seat, looks at me.

"I'm sorry," he says.

"Sure you are," says Dink.

We drive over a flat, smooth road. I can feel comforting vibrations in the seat. Merrit doesn't look too happy.

"I apologize," says Merrit. "Simone Signoret won the Academy Award."

The car drifts in a corner, and as the light passes over the land I can see scrub brush, grayish and brown, like lichen seen through a magnifying glass.

Shhhhh, says Horse-T as we come into the living room. She sleeps in a chair, a magazine open in her lap, one brown, spotted hand comforting another. We walk through the room like considerate sneak thieves. Horse-T's careful with the door, but it slaps softly into its frame, as though out of habit. We stand in hollow sunlight.

Where are you going? she says with sleepy uneasiness.

For a walk, says Horse-T. No place.

I say something about the land. Horse-T laughs, points toward the eastern horizon.

There's a lava flow over there, he says, his finger raised to sky like a brush to canvas. The astronauts ran around in it for a couple of days, just to get the hang of things.

Ragged country, he says. It looks like the moon. About ten miles over.

We walk toward an outbuilding, a low barn. Stone floor and walls, cathedral odors. It's filled with piles of brown, rodent-like potatoes.

You thought about it? I ask.

Sure, Niles, says Horse-T, anything you want. But it ain't going to do any good.

It'll do some good, I say.

*   *   *

A stick rolls against my foot.

"One time," says Dink, in a stage whisper, "I went over to see Merrit."

He leans close to me.

"No one answers the door," says Dink, "but I know someone's there."

Horse-T glances over at Merrit.

"Easy," says Horse-T.

"So I creep around the back of the house and look in the window," says Dink. He pantomimes a little, places a hand above his brow, an observer's flat salute to distance.

I think of Horse-T killing time.

"Stop the car," says Merrit. "Let me out."

"You don't want to do that," I say to him.

Horse-T laughs.

"And what do I see?" says Dink. "Old Merrit. Standing in front of the mirror on the bedroom door. He's naked."

Horse-T doesn't have to listen, but I know he's curious anyway. Old stories, old comfort.

"And he's got his dick in his hand. Stroking it so gently. He's standing on his tiptoes."

Merrit shakes his head, curses open window shades. A stick rolls against my foot.

"He's naked, mind you, except for one thing. . . ."

"Shut your mouth," says Merrit quietly.

"And that's one of his old lady's tit things. He's watching himself in the mirror, right?"

I nod, supply some punctuation.

"In the pouches he's got two big onions. He's rubbing them with the other hand."

Dink elbows me in the ribs. Merrit turns quickly in his seat. I start laughing when I see it's true.

"That right, Merrit," I say. "How was it?"

I laugh when I think of dinner, heads bowed as grace is said, Merrit eyeing a salad.

"You watch him more than once?" I ask Dink.

He laughs too hard, tries not to hear.

"Shut up," says Horse-T to me. He means it.

The road's white perforations flash steadily under the car, line bullets in a child's drawing of war. Horse-T turns onto a side road, one that winds around the only hill within miles. As the road narrows, brush and low branches scrape against the side of the car.

"Quiet now," says Dink. "We don't want to disturb anybody."

We come to the top of the hill, a bald spot.

"There," says Dink, looking into the darkness beyond the window. "There's somebody. Who's that?"

Horse-T's going to find them all, I think, he's got to. I'm not happy about it.

"Shh," says Dink.

Dry sticks and lumps of earth pop beneath the tires. The top of the hill looks like a dark island in a dark sea. At the rim of the plateau there's another car, an old Pontiac, a '52. Indian emblem on the hood. Someone stands behind it, pissing on the bumper. The stream makes a tinkling sound as it strikes the chrome. Dink strains as he moves his bulk through the door.

"How are you, Hoyt?" says Dink to the man behind the Pontiac. "How are you tonight?"

Dink loses his balance for a moment, steadies himself by touching the fender.

"Little better than you," says Hoyt, buttoning his pants as he walks toward us.

"Aw," says Dink, "we're on a party. Getting blasted."

Hoyt sees Horse-T, slaps him on the shoulder, offers his hand.

"Heard you been back," says Hoyt.

Hoyt's short and broad, has a stonecutter's thickness. He's worked in a potato cellar all winter, I think.

"You going to be around long?" he asks Horse-T.

Horse-T shakes his head. No.

"Too bad," says Hoyt. "Ain't been no real cutting-up around here since you left."

Merrit looks toward the Pontiac.

"What you doing?" asks Merrit.

"Getting laid," says Hoyt, buttoning the last button of his pants. "Jud's working on her now."

Dink elbows Merrit in the ribs.

"How's she holding up?" asks Horse-T.

"She's tiring a little," says Hoyt, "but outside of that she's all right."

Dink whispers to Merrit, laughs.

"We flipped for it," says Hoyt. "I got it first."

Merrit and Dink run like escaped convicts across the open space between the Buick and the Pontiac. They grab the Pontiac's bumper.

"Goddamn," says Dink, "you been pissing on this."

He wipes his hands on his pants, and begins to rock the Pontiac up and down, slowly at first, but then more quickly.

"*Swing low, sweet chariot,*" sings Dink, with Merrit joining in, "*coming fo' to carry me home . . . Comming . . . fo' to carry me home. . . .*"

Barroom baritones' catch in their throats as they pump the Pontiac up and down.

You ain't asked about my old man, says Horse-T, getting a little high. You seen everything else, why haven't you asked about that?

On the windowsill next to Horse-T's bed there are some arrowheads and fossils. Horse-T slouches against the wall, blows smoke toward the ceiling, counts the egg boxes. I sit on my bed, opposite him. I hear her in the kitchen, putting pans on the stove.

He's your father, I say, looking at my boots on the floor, pigeon-toed, their tongues hanging out like a dog's.

Horse-T laughs.

He's dead, says Horse-T. He says it like, He's in the other room. I look toward the bedroom door. Horse-T's mother beats on pots in the kitchen, frightens ghosts.

I know, I say. She shows it, the way her hands play with one another.

Horse-T taps the wall with a knuckle.

He hated this place, he says. Jesus, did he hate it! She's tried to fix it up, I think. Horse-T's watching me. I nod.

Now there's bad ways, says Horse-T.

He's watching me. I want to tell him something, want to exchange more than an injury. I think of farm machinery, made to cut.

Horse-T finishes the joint, makes a cocktail out of one of my cigarettes.

He got pulled into a bailer, says Horse-T. Funny thing was, they were trying to get him to a hospital so fast they didn't look for his arm. Never found it.

I think of flesh-eating horses, pleased with what they find in the center of a bail.

"Ain't we got something to do tonight?" I ask Horse-T.

Horse-T watches the car, its rear end bouncing up and down like a retching dog.

"Later, later," says Horse-T. "Too early."

He passes me the bottle.

"Relax," he says.

"Commming. . . . Oh, commming fo' to carry me home."

Dink and Merrit move up and down. Sky is pierced by glowing bits, like a phosphorescent sea. Hoyt takes the bottle out of my hand.

"Who are you?" he asks.

"That's Niles," says Horse-T.

"From Hollywood," screams Dink.

Hoyt grunts, takes a long pull from the bottle, gives it back to me. He's got a round face with two creases, like new moons, on both sides of his lips. Even when he's frowning it looks like he's smiling.

"You showing him the local sights?" he asks Horse-T.

"Local sights," says Horse-T, "right, right."

"Well," says Hoyt, "there's going to be one coming out of that Pontiac in about a minute. Good thing I set the brake or they would have pushed 'er right over the edge."

Horse-T taps a single knuckle against the wall.

You thought about it? I ask.

Sure, he says, anything you want. But it ain't going to do any good.

It'll do some good, I say.

Horse-T finishes his cocktail, puts the cigarette out on a fossil.

You know, Niles, says Horse-T, my old man built that trestle. It was his idea.

Dink stops pumping, turns away from the car, and retches. He doesn't bother to bend over or anything, he just blows vomit into the air and jumps back from it. He touches his lips with the back of his hand, then turns to the Pontiac.

"Ain't we got something to do?" I say quietly to Horse-T. "Ain't we?"

"Later," says Horse-T. "We got to wait."

Hoyt looks at me suspiciously.

"Wait?" I ask, knowing why, but unable to stop. "Wait for what? People go to bed around here as soon as it gets dark."

"There's a watchman," says Horse-T, "but he usually goes to sleep around eleven."

Bullshit, I think, bullshit.

"Ain't any reason to have all these people along, either," I say.

"Easy, Niles," says Horse-T.

"There ain't any watchman," I say.

Horse-T shrugs.

I wait for local sights.

"I seen enough," I say, getting angry, already feeling bad for it, knowing it's wrong.

"But I haven't," says Horse-T.

I light a cigarette, cup my fingers around the match, make a jack-o'-lantern of my hands. Horse-T sees that for a moment I'm frightened.

"All right," I mumble. "Okay."

Springs in the Pontiac creak.

"Here he comes," says Hoyt. "Ain't he the happy one, though?"

Horse-T smiles.

"Sure," says Horse-T. "Hope he doesn't kill somebody."

The door of the Pontiac swings open quickly, but Merrit, who's on the driver's side, doesn't hear or see it. He just keeps pumping. Dink sees it and jumps back, laughing. Jud runs quickly along the side of the Pontiac, takes two long strides, then kicks at the bumper, catches Merrit's hand against the chrome. Pontiac shifts on its springs, creaks. Merrit stands quickly, cradles one hand in another, steps back. I can't see his face, but I know he looks surprised. Merrit takes another step, begins to say something, but it doesn't matter because Jud swings, hits Merrit, knocks him down. Dink laughs. I can hear that sound, like someone kicking a football that's only half-inflated. Dink laughs. Merrit's head hits the fender, and then he rolls behind the Pontiac. He tries to stand, supports himself on all fours, puts his hand in the puddle of piss.

"Jud ain't mad," says Hoyt. "He's having too good a time."

Horse-T nods. He looks toward the Pontiac with mug-shot eyes.

Dink pushes Jud on top of Merrit, and they roll over one another in the dry grass, their boots making flat sounds as they hit the hard earth. Dink kicks at both of them, but I can see that he kicks Merrit a lot harder.

"You prick, you son of a bitch," says Jud, laughing. "I ought to kill you."

He points at Dink, who's standing behind the Pontiac.

"You, too," he says.

The girl, sitting in the front seat of the car, rolls the window down. I can see her resting her head and arm against the door. She ignores the voices from the rear of the Pontiac, not caring what is said.

"We was just helping you out," says Dink.

"Sure," says Jud, standing up. He has the lankiness of a baseball pitcher. "Just what I need. Couple of lunatics helping me get fucked."

But Merrit isn't laughing. He stands next to the Pontiac, his hands on his knees, breathing deeply. I know how hard Dink kicked him.

"You know it ain't ever been so good," says Dink. "Ain't that the truth?"

Jud smells his hands, feels that the back of his shirt is wet, and shakes his head with disbelief.

"And," says Dink, "you got some real nice oh de cologne."

I watch the girl resting her head on her arm.

"Christ," says Jud, seeing Horse-T, "you out here, too?"

He offers Horse-T his hand.

"Heard you been back," says Jud.

Horse-T doesn't like greetings. Jud's smile hangs on his face a moment too long. He has nothing more to say.

"Christ," says Jud.

Merrit begins to cough, then retches. He spits into the weeds.

"What's the matter, Merrit, baby?" says Dink. "Sounds like you're puking."

Merrit spits into the weeds.

I look at the girl, realize how comfortable she is in the front seat of that Pontiac. Horse-T follows me as I walk to the car. She has short, dark hair with spit curls, held together with small alligator clips, over her ears.

"How are you tonight?" asks Horse-T, trying to be courtly, with a half-empty bottle in his hand.

She lifts her head from her arms. I can see full breasts with broad bases, the soft flesh on the inside of her thigh. She sits on a seat covered with plastic plaid.

"This is Niles," says Horse-T.

She looks at me and smiles.

Horse-T's curious, too, even though he's had her a hundred times.

"Something's torn," says Merrit in a hissing whisper. "I can feel it."

"Yeah?" says Dink with the beginnings of a fatherly concern. "Where?"

Dink walks through the grass with an unsure, splayed gait, as though he carried his bulk on his shoulder.

"It burns," says Merrit. "Jesus, doesn't it burn when I breathe!"

She smiles. That's right, I think, that's fine. Front seat of a Pontiac. Indian emblem on the hood. I lean against the side of the car, touch her arm. She doesn't pull away.

"Let me see," says Dink. "Where's it hurt?"

Merrit pulls up his shirt, points out the spot.

"There," says Merrit, "something's torn. I can feel a loose end."

Her hair is stiff, spray-laminated, smells like a drugstore's cosmetics counter. She smiles. I feel small-town nostalgia, though I haven't been in many. Jud sees me touch her arm.

"You want a drink?" says Horse-T, offering the bottle. She shakes her head.

"No," she says, "no. I don't want any of that."

I listen to the sound of Jud's boots moving in the grass behind me. Dink, with a pistol finger, touches Merrit's stomach.

"There?" he says. "There?"

I listen to the boots, then look at the girl and feel myself getting hard. Jud shifts his weight. I'm going to give him a new mouth, I think, holding the bottle, I'm going to let him scream.

"You mean right up here," says Dink.

"Yeah."

The girl senses something: she thinks with her eyes. I

hear her laugh, sounds from a rough throat. Hoyt walks in the weeds somewhere off to my left.

"What you going to do tonight?" Jud asks Horse-T.

"Get lost," I say.

Horse-T laughs, makes Jud unsure.

Dink fingers the spot just beneath the breastbone.

"Gee," says Dink, "that's too bad. Didn't think I kicked you that hard."

Quickly and easily Dink's fingers curl into a fist. He drops his weight behind his arm and hits Merrit. Where Merrit said it burned. Merrit looks surprised, standing there, holding up his shirt. He falls backward, as though he had been pushed into a swimming pool. The weeds surround him when he hits the ground, like a splash caught in a still photograph.

"You son of a bitch," screams Dink, "you lying bastard."

Merrit rolls in the weeds, kicks at Dink, then trips him. They roll over one another in the grass.

"If it didn't hurt before," says Merrit, "it sure does now."

Both of them begin to laugh.

I listen to the boots moving in the grass as Horse-T looks at me, slowly shaking his head. She smiled when I touched her arm. Horse-T's curiosity is satisfied, but mine isn't. He's angry, robbed of nostalgia, a saving grace. I reach for the door handle.

"Race! Race! Race!" yells Hoyt.

She frowns, jerks her head toward the voice, then squeezes my arm. Jud begins to run around the front of the Pontiac, trying to get to the door on the driver's side. I hear his hand slap the hood. Hoyt's already in the car.

"Come on," says Horse-T.

We run, too, except Horse-T's careless, steps into some brush, falls. I stop to help him.

"Go on!" he says, pointing toward the Buick. "Go on!"

Merrit runs through the scrub brush.

"Fuck," says Horse-T. "The keys are in the ignition."

I run straight out, trying to catch Merrit. Horse-T jumps and begins to run after me, but he moves a lot slower. Merrit reaches the Buick, swings open the door, and climbs into the driver's seat.

In the Pontiac I can see Jud push Hoyt next to and then on top of the girl. The car sounds like a piece of farm machinery, starts with a steady popping. Headlights illuminate the air beyond the plateau.

"Merrit," yells Horse-T angrily, "Merrit!"

The Buick's engine turns over, then catches, pushes heavy exhaust over the weeds, makes them pulse stiffly. Merrit pulls the car into gear as I climb into the right-hand seat. Horse-T manages to open the back door and pull himself in, too, just as Merrit takes off. But Dink doesn't. I see him running, pinned against the night by the headlights. Pontiac's got a chipped gear.

Clink. Clink. Clink.

Counterpoint to the engine's steady popping as the Pontiac bounces over a rut, heads across the open space toward the road. Merrit spins the wheel like a submarine hatch screw, then pushes his foot to the floor. Buick makes a graceful half circle, slides over the grass. Scrub brush claws the underbody. I can feel it with my feet.

"Easy, Merrit," says Horse-T, "you just take it easy."

Headlights shine on Dink's face, touch his skin with a garish cosmetic. He still runs toward us, dodging the Pontiac, which bounces past him onto the beginning of the dirt road. The weeds beyond it are slippery, deep.

"You watch out for him," says Horse-T. Homecoming, homecoming. "You look out for him. . . ."

Tires burn in the grass, then grip. Dink laughs, runs toward us, makes spastic toreador gestures. I reach for the keys, try to switch off the engine, but Merrit puts the car into another half circle. I'm thrown against the door. Dink senses something in the way the car comes toward him, and begins to move backward over tire-ironed weeds, trying to keep his balance, tripping over a rut. The taillights of the Pontiac disappear around the first turn, a dragon's eyes as it backs into its lair. Dink jumps up, back-pedals, always watching the Buick as it skids over the grass, moving like an animal's tail. I reach for the keys, catch hold of them, switch off the engine as Dink reaches the gravel road, turns, and begins to run. He trips over the hump between the ruts, a long island covered with grass. I feel the quiet resistance of heavy, oiled steel. The Buick breathes steadily as it coasts, cylinders sucking air. As Dink falls he twists onto his back so he can watch the Buick. Something rolls in the back seat.

One thump. Just one. I can feel it in the Buick's frame. Dink's face disappears beneath the hood, his eyes, gelatinous sacs, filled with light.

"Stupid cock-sucker," says Horse-T.

Merrit sits as still as a dummy in an automotive safety test.

Merrit's one sick-looking bastard. Dummy's good looks. Dink's lying just behind the front wheel, holding one leg, using the other to push himself away from the car.

"Shit!" says Dink. He uses his arms to pull himself through the weeds.

"Don't go moving around," I say. "If it's broken you don't want to twist it."

"Broken, shit," says Dink. "It ain't broken."

"Sure," I say.

"He ran right over me, didn't he, Niles?"

"Looks like it," I say.

They never went this far before, Niles, thinks Horse-T, that's it.

He's gentle as he feels Dink's knee.

"We got to roll up his pant leg, or cut it, or something," says Horse-T.

Merrit's still in the Buick.

"Naw," says Dink, "you don't have to cut it."

From the car Horse-T takes a box cutter, a razor in a handle covered with small pyramids.

"You don't have to cut it, Niles," says Dink, "you don't have to."

I touch the leg where he's been holding it, at the knee. There's swelling under the heavy cloth.

Horse-T holds the box cutter over the knee.

"Naw," says Dink, "you don't have to cut it. Come on now."

I hold the cloth taut. You can hear every thread as the blade cuts toward the boot.

"Some party," says Dink.

"Shut up," says Horse-T.

Dink looks like a prisoner being prepared for the chair. I roll back the cloth and see in light from the Buick's headlamp a joint that looks like a large pink cantaloupe. Most of the skin's torn away where the tire's edge spun.

"Look at that," says Dink. He lifts the flap of skin, looks at the greasy meat inside.

I'm tired. Damp clothes cling to me like an old man's skin. Horse-T's mother bumps into me, apologizes, then pretends I'm not in the house. I wait at the kitchen counter while the water runs cold, a stolen A & W root beer mug in my hand. The sink's been cleaned so many times some of the porcelain has been worn away, exposing spots of black metal underneath. It looks like the skin of a Dalmatian. I take a long drink, let some of the water run out of the corners of my mouth onto the front of my shirt, feel spongy muscles jump at its coldness. Horse-T's mother turns for a moment, sees me, smiles. She approves. The baptism of a hard day's work. For a moment I lose my strangeness, become one of her own. There's something odd about the water. After you've swallowed, your mouth suddenly feels dry. Horse-T comes in the door behind us, his boots playing the wooden floor like a drum.

Water drips from my face. Horse-T sees me grimace, then laughs.

Something gets into the water, he says, from that trestle. Creosote, maybe.

The Pontiac's lights cut the trees from the sky. We hear it climbing to the top of the hill again, its popping engine and that chipped gear.

Merrit still sits in the Buick.

"Should be something on it," says Horse-T, watching Dink hold the flap of skin between his thumb and forefinger.

I take a drink from the bottle, then begin to pour it over the knee.

"Not that," says Horse-T.

Dink mutters foolishly.

The Pontiac stops in front of us, catches us in a crossfire of lights. My shadow goes both ways, cut down the middle. Horse-T squints, waves the Pontiac onto the grass. The doors slam. Hoyt and Jud stand behind us. Pastoral chess pieces. Hoyt looks more at me than at the cut.

"Hey, Merrit," I say, "get a look at this."

Horse-T touches my arm, shakes his head.

"You seen enough?" I whisper to Horse-T.

"He run me over," says Dink to Hoyt and Jud.

They look at the knee, the meat.

"Doesn't look like you're going to die," says Hoyt.

"Die, shit," says Dink. "Take more than that to kill me."

Everyone laughs except Dink.

"You don't understand," says Dink. "He run me over!"

Dink insists, almost certain, almost flattered. Horse-T sees it, too, and winces.

"You got something to put on it?" says Horse-T.

Dink tries not to smile. Horse-T looks away from him.

"Some mouthwash in the glove box," says Hoyt. He gestures toward the Pontiac with his shoulder.

"I'll get it," I say.

She rests her head and arms on the door of the Pontiac, her face turned away from me. I can't help swaggering, walking with a sea-rolling gait. She finds it difficult to pose, nestles her head into her arms. Pontiac's beached on a slight grade near the edge of the plateau, surrounded by wind-drifted weeds, branches. One wheel's almost off the ground. Frame ticks with the strain. Stretched shadows of my legs move across the side of the car, over her.

"Merrit!" screams Dink.

"Shut up," says Horse-T.

"I'm going to kick his ass," says Dink.

The others stand around him as though he were a small fire.

"What you want?" she says, quickly turning her face toward me. Her hand moves across the seat, touches something, stops. The air is cool, makes me know the lines of my face. She looks toward the others, senses their anger, knows by it she wasn't sold. She smiles. I open the door, touch her, feel warm skin, her stiff and lacquered hair. She sits up, tolerates the open door, me standing there. Pontiac's filled with her sweet and fishy smell.

"What do you want in here?" she says.

Hoyt stands with his hands in his pockets, rocking slightly on his heels. He glances away from Dink, the wound.

Mud sucks at my shoes as I walk in the ditch at the side of the road. A column, white as Grecian marble, turns gray as the lights of the car pass away from it. Layered, feathering water moves across the asphalt, slithers against a high-tide mark, a sloppy dam of broken posts as thick as telephone poles, sheets of metal, torn planks. Ears are numb, asleep, filled with a sound that matches the rough hissing of the water as it falls to the road. A plank pulses against the ridge of trash. Just a plank. Undulating in the flat current that moves across the road. The column turns red, but fades again as the car, its brake lights, move quickly up the road. Just a plank. I'm not a mariner, don't know the constellations, can't find the southern stars. Mud sucks at my boots, makes the senile sound of a toothless man slurping his soup. The car is gone.

New car, says Horse-T. Nothing she likes better than a new car.

Fucking new car.

Plank pulses against the ridge of trash. Bits of metal burrow in skin, add an ounce or two. I become angry, then afraid of wandering onto the surface of the moon where the astronauts walked.

* * *

"What you want in here?" she says.

She's comfortable with her body, lets it rest easily, her legs open a little, skirt above her knees. I reach over her, open the glove box. Tinny, loose sound as the small door slaps against the stops of its hinges. White skin shines in diffused light. I lean over her carefully, let my side touch only her shoulder, breasts, arm. Bottle rattles against the pasteboard sides of the glove box. She looks over her shoulder, sees the angry faces around Dink. I begin to stand, slap the small door closed. She watches herself as I run my hand across her breasts, as I move them easily in her blouse, then touch the inside of her thigh, the slick flesh there, the flat place between her legs. I catch her head, hold a fistful of black, lacquered hair, run my tongue along her neck. I bite her, taste her, think of drawing blood. My hand touches something, a rag, her underwear, and her wetness, too, where she's dripped on the seat. She spreads her legs, puts one foot over the drive-shaft hump. I feel tendons, muscles on the inside of her thigh become rigid, sharp near the groin, framing clipped torso, dark hair. Open blisters, torn skin on my hand are soothed by warmth and moisture, her soft pressure, the light touch of hair. She pulls her skirt beneath her buttocks, brings her heels to the edge of the seat, watches me, pushes a knee against my shoulder. I feel affectionate for a moment, kiss her face, eyelids, hairline, then think of marking her. Outside, by the car, the Buick, someone yells, but she doesn't hear.

"Hey," she says, "are you really from Hollywood?"

I begin to laugh. She closes her thighs tightly: her slow embarrassment grows. I close the Pontiac's door, turn and walk down the slight grade, catch my foot in a rut and fall, still laughing. That's right, sure. I chew a long black cigar, push it into the corner of my mouth, and whisper, when I can breathe, "That's right, baby. Get you a scream test."

Hoyt hears me laughing, and takes a step away from the circle around Dink.

"What's so funny?" he asks Horse-T.

Horse-T looks at me, then shrugs.

"Bring that shit over here," he says.

I swagger down the slope.

"Here it is," I say.

I hold the bottle to the light, look at the contents, a bright red watery fluid that looks like thin blood. It splashes over the wound.

"That smarts some," says Dink.

"What's so funny?" asks Hoyt.

Bright fluid runs down Dink's leg.

"It's not getting inside," I say.

Horse-T gently lifts the flap of skin, exposing the meat. I pour the fluid into the wound.

"Smarts . . ." says Dink.

Merrit's still sitting in the car. I take the bottle of bourbon from Horse-T, have a long pull, then offer it to Dink, hold it under his nose so he can smell my fingers.

"Hey," I say to Horse-T, "guess what?"

Horse-T tries to pull the edges of the jeans together, but he's watching Hoyt.

"You know what?" I ask. "She wants to know where I come from."

But she already knows: I breathe electricity, feed on the bones of star beasts, pick my teeth with meteorites. A galactic desperado. Horse-T hears me laughing, but he doesn't look at me. He's watching Hoyt's hands.

"Someone's got to take Dink home," says Horse-T.

Dink's got the edges of the cloth bunched together in his fist trying to hold it together.

"Naw," says Dink. "I don't want to go home. Party's just getting started."

"You take him home?" asks Horse-T.

Give me a chance, you mother-fuckers.

Hoyt looks at us for a moment, then says, "I guess so."

"Christ on a crutch," says Dink. "Haven't . . ."

But Hoyt and Jud are already walking, their shadows clipped by the end of the plateau, the sky. They speak angrily to one another, then turn on the girl when they open the Pontiac's door. But she's no slouch. She may be bored, but she carries their scars. It doesn't take long. Hoyt and Jud are quiet.

"Some party," says Dink, still holding the edges of the cloth together.

Horse-T looks at me suspiciously when he sees I am disappointed.

"No need," says Horse-T, "no need at all, Niles."

Clink. Clink. Clink.

Pontiac stops next to us. She sits on her right side, smoking a cigarette, sneaking unsure glances at me. We open the door, then strain against Dink's bulk, the stench of vomit. He catches a foot on the doorframe, laughs as we struggle to make him comfortable, to prop him against the side panel of the back seat.

"You tell him for me, Niles," says Dink. He points toward the Buick. "You tell him."

I rest my hand on the front seat, on her shoulder. Hoyt and Jud stare straight ahead.

Horse-T grabs me, pulls me from the car.

Mud sucks at my shoes. I can't see it, but I know what it looks like, that trestle, a black insect, its back broken, leaking clear, vital juices. I say something about the land and Horse-T points to the east. Road runs north and south, it's got to, because there's only one other and that comes from the east, Idaho, Montana, Wyoming.

Niles, Horse-T says to me, I haven't changed any, I've just forgotten something about being alive. Jesus, I had it, Niles, you should have seen me.

But when we came in, I think, listening to the water hit the road, we came to a junction, didn't we? Which means this road runs east-west. Horse-T pointed to the east. Something moves in the pile of trash. I turn quickly toward it, run a step or two, then stop. But I don't know whether I'm east or west of the junction.

I hear a cog searching in a broken gear. As the Pontiac turns onto the gravel road Hoyt looks at me so there'll be no mistake. He sticks his middle finger into the air.

"Local sights," says Horse-T.

Pontiac moves like an amphibian, sliding slowly into the ruts. I can hear her scream, angry with seminal insults, the prospect of riding a bastard nine months. She squeezed my arm.

"They were showing off for you," I say to him, "that's all."

"Sure," says Horse-T, knowing I've seen too much.

Horse-T throws the empty bottle toward the edge of the plateau, listens to the mouth as it sings in the air.

"There's another in the car," he says.

"What about him?" I ask.

Horse-T shrugs, looks toward the car.

"He can come along."

Buick's desolate-looking, doors open, lights on. Merrit must be lying in the back seat. Looks like a flying saucer landed, carried off driver and passengers. On one side of the plateau I see a nesting place in the sinewy brush.

"You know," I say, "you know we're going to have to make ourselves pretty scarce. Some people around here ain't going to be exactly pleased."

"Sure," he says. "Hope Merrit hasn't found that other bottle."

In the Gulf, I think, we'll catch fish as big as a bus, swim naked at night with the whores, lick rum from their flesh. Farmer will moan in the lining.

"We can be in Frisco by morning, L.A. by . . ."

"Shut up," says Horse-T.

We walk toward the Buick.

"You got any Indians around here?" I ask.

Horse-T laughs.

"Sure we do, Niles," he says. "We got Klamath Indians. Crazy fuckers, too."

Merrit smiles at us when we climb into the Buick, but I can see he's been crying.

"There's a killing a week over in Klamath Falls," says Horse-T, "mostly in movie theaters."

I think for a moment of Indians, stalking the aisles, knives in hand, their enemies in velvet seats.

"You ever use this stuff?" asks Horse-T.

"No," I say.

"Where arc wc going?" asks Merrit.

"Relax," says Horse-T.

"Sure," says Merrit. "Just thought I'd ask. . . ."

"You'll show me?" I ask. I hold a stick, a piece of paper, and wax fruit, but it's got a rotten spot, a bruise, broken formula. The cross section of fuse looks like a small target, a dark bull's-eye in the center. From the box Horse-T takes a blasting cap, a silver bullet, and works the fuse into its lip. He crimps the lip over the fuse.

"Just squeeze the lip, Niles," says Horse-T, "never the cap itself."

Horse-T's fingers move like a logger's legs over the pile of sticks.

"There's some billboards, you know, big ones . . ." says Merrit, trying to join. Schoolboy pranks.

Horse-T holds the pliers at their crotch and, using the end of one grip, pierces the stick twice, once all the way through, once halfway.

"You see, Niles, you got to make two holes."

The capped fuse looks like a black snake with a silver head. Horse-T pushes it into the first hole, the one that goes all the way through, and draws it out the other side. Like sewing.

"Was Dink hurt?" asks Merrit.

Horse-T pushes the cap into the other hole, into the center of the stick. Looks like black snake's burrowing, trying to cover himself.

"See that, Niles?" says Horse-T, holding it out for me, slowly turning it back and forth like a product on mechanical display. "This way you can throw it. The fuse won't fall off."

Horse-T drops it into my hand. It has a vain weight, like a shotgun.

"See?" says Horse-T. "And if you need more than one, you tape them together. This one'll set off the rest."

They have a distinct smell, the stick and fuse, like a new car.

"Did you have to cut his pants?" asks Merrit.

If you need more than one . . .

"Come on," says Horse-T, stepping out of the car. "We'll see if this shit is any good."

When we stand at the end of the plateau, I put the fuse into Horse-T's cupped hands, where the match burns. Horse-T doesn't have to tell me twice to throw it.

Muffled slap of muscle and bone. We watch it fall, the fuse burning, a slow-moving pinwheel.

I open the car door.

"Looks like it works," says Horse-T.

Merrit looks beyond the lip of the plateau. All of us smell it. Vain and clean. Merrit rolls up the window.

"Merrit?" asks Horse-T.

The water is only a trickle now, a few drops, fluid clappers that fall on a piece of corrugated aluminum. There was grass in the bottom of the pipe, the kind with long green strands, and bits of it cling to debris, shrapnel, trash in the road. I saw it by the car's light, its roots with small suckers that turned the aluminum white where they were attached, as though they fed on metal alone. Strands of it cling to my clothes. I think, I've got to think, if the water's stopped running, I can't stay here. There's enough water in that reservoir to run for a year, so it couldn't have stopped by itself. Valve's been closed. I walk along the road, quiet as an Indian, my shoes covered with doughy mud, but I become frightened, think for a moment of running into the bushes, hiding there. It doesn't matter, I tell myself carefully, I'll be able to see the lights. If they're driving.

There's a watchman, says Horse-T.

Bullshit, I say, there ain't any watchman.

Watchman would be on foot. But he'd carry a lantern, all watchmen carry lanterns. The police should be driving. I'm angry, knowing I've made a mistake, that I'm walking the wrong way, that this road runs east-west, that I'm walking away from the junction of the north-south road. Horse-T pointed east, to the moon.

"Merrit?" asks Horse-T.

"Yeah," says Merrit. "It looks like it works."

* * *

Near the bottom of the hill, light passes over flat land, scrub brush, jack-lighted rabbits, their eyes metallic membranes, softened and diffused by vitreous humor, corona smears. Horse-T lifts his hands from the wheel, watches the way the ruts steer the car. I can't see the tops of the telephone poles when we turn onto the main road, but I'm pleased with the idea they've been blown away, leaving splintered stumps above the light. Horse-T's hands, small monsters, hang from the steering wheel, guide us through a lazy turn. Turn? Ain't any need for a turn. Land's flat, nothing to avoid, no gullies, hills, dry stream beds. Engineer says, explaining an indulgence, people fall asleep on a road that hasn't got any curves. Don't worry, friend. I'm awake. Flat land makes me nervous.

But there's a ridge, a wrinkle in flat land, and the road cuts through it. That's where the trestle is. It looks like a black centipede, its back arched over the road, legs, spin, primitive armor made from metal and planks, posts. It stinks of creosote, wood's embalming fluid.

Horse-T turns off the lights.

Cut from the sky, against the stars, I can see the ridge, the break in it.

"We want to do this quickly," says Horse-T. "No need to hang around."

"That?" says Merrit.

"Right, right," says Horse-T.

Car sways like a lizard walking down a rock as Horse-T drives through the highway's median to turn around.

"You want to make it," says Horse-T, "like I showed you?"

The tires spin at the bottom of the median, make a rubbery screech, a diminished siren. Car stumbles. I feel that shoulder go down, but then we climb to the road, a comforting surface.

"You'll wait here," I say to Merrit.

Horse-T drives by braille, listens for the gravel on the shoulder of the road. I think of the sound, am aware of four turning places, pinwheels with firestones, sparks.

"He should be able to see well enough from here," I say.

Horse-T looks angrily at me.

"But he's got to see," I say, "doesn't he?"

Don't worry about details, mug-shot injuries, cruel stories, I think. Even insult will make us lonely.

"You got to see what you're doing, Niles," he says, flicking on the dashlight. I feel the pliers squeeze through the fuse, a soft click. I think of a clock, cutting it like a pie.

"Be quick about it, Niles," he says. "Someone comes along now and they're going to stop."

"You shouldn't have cut those pants," says Merrit. "He ain't got anyone to sew them."

Don't worry about those pants. It feels good to crimp the cap over the end of the fuse. Like biting a piece of soft metal. Don't worry about those pants.

"He's got somebody," I say absentmindedly. Merrit doesn't hear me, and I'm glad.

"How many?" I ask.

"Well," says Horse-T, "we only got one chance. . . ."

I tear tape from the roll, make a sound like a butcher ripping fat and membrane from cold meat. I tape all of them together. The bundle looks unmanufactured, jerry-made, but it's heavy, complete.

Horse-T doesn't wait. I hear the door slam, look up and see he's gone. One key is in the ignition. The others swing back and forth on a chain of tiny balls. Merrit eyes them.

"You weren't planning on going anywhere, were you?" I ask, taking the keys.

Merrit looks up when I close the door. It's a whole, solid sound, as though the car were an icebox. Merrit's lips move behind the glass.

"Turn off the lights!" I say.

He mouths something behind the glass in the greenish, aquatic light from the dashboard.

"He wasn't mad!" I scream.

I can feel the trestle pressing against the air, and I can smell the water as it runs in the open, corrugated pipe. Horse-T's boots kick gravel.

"Wait a minute," I say.

Gravel rests.

"Here I am," says Horse-T. His arm touches my elbow. Eyes suck night, become filled, vacuum-cleaner eyes.

"You left the keys in the car," I say.

I drop them into his shirt pocket. Horse-T begins to laugh.

"It doesn't matter," he says. "There's another set. In a magnet box, beneath the dash."

I develop the night slowly, see it, back arched over the road, the four lanes.

"But if it will make you feel better," says Horse-T, "I'll go back and get those, too."

"No," I say.

I wanted him to think about later. He doesn't think we'll need that Buick.

"You shouldn't have left those keys," I say angrily.

Horse-T laughs.

"Right, right," he says.

I touch the first pole, one of the ten or so that are close to the road, one of those that are covered with tin can reflectors. People around here don't want some farmer Cadillacing down the road and smacking right into it. We stand beneath the trestle, looking for a place to climb. I can feel it above us, its presence in the air, a primitive cathedral. The poles are dry and fissured, streaked here and there with slime, and as we walk my fingers play across them. I think of the vital, frightening moisture left by space monsters. Water drops onto my head, back, shoulders. It stings because it's fallen so far. Scalp feels as though drops of cold silver have fallen there. Horse-T moves from pole to pole, trying to find climbing pegs, aluminum L's that have been driven into the wood.

I hate the smell of creosote.

In the median, mud makes molds of our feet. Cops will be pleased, will bring plaster of paris to make fossils of our soles. Water, like a marionette's string, makes Horse-T bunch his shoulders together with a spastic shrug.

"Shit," says Horse-T, wiping the back of his neck.

Water drips.

"Well?" I say.

Horse-T strains against the mud, walks like a man in a windstorm. I can hear its slimy grip.

Water drips.

"Well?" I say.

Horse-T moves from pole to pole, frisking each one.

"I can't find them," he says.

But he goes on looking, just the same.

"Forget it," I say, "it doesn't matter."

"The hell!" says Horse-T.

Water drips.

"I've got to carry this," I say, holding out the bundle. "I can't climb."

Horse-T becomes ashamed, sees I'm watching his closed fist.

"You could put it in your shirt," he says quietly, "tuck it in tight."

I shake my head.

"Well . . . ?" says Horse-T.

"I can't climb."

He follows as I walk across the road, its surface still day-warm, soothing. Brush breaks against us, cuts, crackles as we stalk the ridge where the top of the trestle rests. Dirt and pebbles slither downhill in a dry lava flow that makes a sandy hiss in the gully. The mud on our boots becomes dusty, takes a chalky skin. We look misshapen, hobbling along on grayish lumps of flesh. Brush sonar, an even crackling.

"Shit," says Horse-T. He stumbles, grunts, then catches a branch. "Some fine idea this is, Niles."

I smell the torn limbs, the brush's milky sap, and the dust, too.

"Up here," I say.

Horse-T breaks through, and I see on his face a streak of black blood. The railroad ties are just above my head, and I put the bundle on them. It rests there like a rat with a long shiny tail. Boots find their way into a joint between post and cross support, a sharp V. The ties are about a foot and a half apart, and between them I see moving water, black silk. Stars are smeared on its surface.

"Good way to break a leg," says Horse-T, pointing to the spaces between the ties.

We walk across the trestle, but with a strained cadence, like walking on a sidewalk without stepping on the cracks. We've got to be over the middle. If we're over the middle it'll fall on the road. Horse-T walks ahead of me, his arms out, pretending he's on a tightrope.

"This looks about right," says Horse-T. "Here. Right here."

"No," I say, pointing toward the middle. My hand's a lump, the bundle. "further up."

"Right, right," says Horse-T, "further up."

Matches rattle in their box. When I see the road's markings, white perforations, I think for a moment of ripping it in half. Bits of mud from my boots fall into the water, disperse the stars.

When the cars pass, their sirens wailing, I'm crouching in a ditch, shivering, wondering if I'd be warmer without my shirt, without wet cloth on my back. I count my steps, calculate the number of them in a mile. Horse-T pointed to the east.

About ten miles. The astronauts ran around over there to get the hang of things.

Fifteen hundred steps makes a mile. If it's less than ten miles, I'll know pretty soon. I take off my pants and shirt, walk to the side of the road, rub myself with dust there. It's dry and still a little warm from the sun. Shivering stops. Car passes, its spotlight dissolving in the bushes where I hide. I wear a gray skin, marred here and there with curdled stains, silt mixed with blood. Spotlight looks like a galactic ship's ray. But the dust is gray. If it's gray, that means I'm heading east, toward the moon. Stiff branches scrape my sides, buttocks, penis, legs, make me feel vulnerable. Skin flinches at the wet cloth as I pull my clothes on. Farmer will be all right, towed to a bone yard, sold for twenty bucks. I walk again, counting my steps, angry because the junction is behind me, in the other direction.

"How about this?" says Horse-T, "this suit you?"
I hand Horse-T the matches. He kneels.

"Sure," I say.

"I'm not taking another step," says Horse-T.

"It's all right," I say.

I kneel opposite Horse-T.

"Before taking another step," says Horse-T, "I'll throw your ass off and go home."

Horse-T's got something in his eye. He holds the matchbox upside down, pushes out the small cardboard drawer. Matches scatter over the tie.

"Shit," says Horse-T, picking one of them up, "when I light it, you drop it right down there."

Small sparks hiss among stars in the water.

"Drop it down," says Horse-T, "drop it down!"

Fuse burns, gives my hand an orange skin. I watch the bundle, a small animal with a burning tail, bounce on the platform beneath the pipe.

"You better run, Niles," says Horse-T.

We start: muffled slap of muscle and bone, boots against wood.

"Niles!"

I step between the ties. Cold water fills my boot.

"Niles!"

Horse-T stands against skeletal sky, illuminated mist. White water rises like a time-lapse flower. Bits of metal, each a different size, spin through ruptured air, each making a different sound. Chunks of post, fireplace size, twist in the air, then land around us like maces with bolt spikes. The trestle quakes, lifts, and collapses in the middle. It drops about ten feet or so, then catches on its beams and cross supports, wobbles from side to side. Horse-T screams. Sections of pipe, timbers, planks, pieces of tin drop to the road in a regular cadence. Tiny bits of metal, those that were blown the highest, begin to fall: a sharp and shiny rain. From somewhere, the

ridge, sky, there's a sluggish echo. Water in the pipe
begins to move faster, pulls at my leg. The trestle settles
a little more, its ruptured underbelly slipping in the
harsh support of torn posts and planks. I can hear them
crack under the strain. Horse-T tries to stand, falls, rolls
over a broken tie, then catches a naked bolt. The trestle
slants steeply toward the center of the road, over which
there's a break, a ragged hole. I sit as though on a
seesaw, afraid to move, afraid the trestle could fall to
the highway. The last of the water settles over in a
soothing mist. Horse-T stands on wobbling planks, takes
an involuntary step backward, supports himself with
one hand. I try to help, but he shakes his head, ashamed
and mystified by exposed viscera. Water bleeds, turns
white as it's clawed by the pipe's curled edge. Horse-T
makes a perfect gesture, steps backward, and falls
through the ragged hole.

I run to the ridge, watching in the light from the
Buick a steady tide moving across the road, pushing
shattered posts into a high tide line at the side of the
highway. A plank, probably a plank, bounces in the
water, oddly buoyant.

The Buick moves up the road, its headlights illumi-
nating the falling water, a Grecian column, cut from
marble.

I find him near the ditch, one arm animated by water, his brow wet and clean. The quarter moon of timbers creaks in the steady tide. I pull him to a dry spot on
the shoulder of the road and feel, like broken tiles in a
sack, the bones at the back of his head.

The Buick stops near us, just back from the water.

"Don't look at me!" I scream.

I try to hold the back of the head together.

"Don't look at me!"

* * *

The gray dust is light, and it smells like pumice stone.
I walk the lunar landscape, carefully picking my way
among gray boulders, feeling their pocked surface with
my hand. Strange creatures, slimy from the larvae, claw
gray stones, follow me with plasma eyes. I violate their
breeding grounds, step on the cold and brittle eggs
hidden in small caves, on the edge of a crater, beneath
the dust. Predawn breezes hiss among the stones. It's
still too dark to see what flies, but I hear crinkling wings
and smell the nauseating odor in the air. I climb a boul-
der, search a constricted horizon of shattered rock, wait
for daylight. Small dust storms race toward the center
of a crater as I walk along its sharp and final edge.
Something digs beneath the dust. There is cool and
brackish fluid in a stone's pock, and it soothes my face
and arms.

I wander far from the shore, onto a lunar sea where I
am caught, exposed by the dawn, a rising monster in
the east.